SUPERIOR PERIL

MURDER
ON 123

BY MICHAEL CARRIER

A number of very wonderful people helped me prepare the contents of this book. Each of them contributed significantly. Thank you Evie, Meredith, Charity, Steve, Jeff, and special thanks to George and Gay. And thanks to Lora for her helpful advice on the cover.

SUPERIOR

PERIL

MURDER
ON 123

MICHAEL CARRIER

GREENWICH VILLAGE INK

GRAND RAPIDS, MICHIGAN

SUPERIOR PERIL

SUPERIOR PERIL—Murder on 123. Copyright 2013 by Michael Carrier.

Published 2013 by Greenwich Village Ink, Grand Rapids, MI.

Visit the JACK website at http://www.greenwichvillageink.com/galleria-1.2.9/galleria/themes/classic/peril.htm.
For additional information (and sometimes puzzles) visit JACK's blog: http://jackhandlerny.blogspot.com/.

Author can be emailed at michael.jon.carrier@gmail.com.

ISBN: 978-1-936092-27-7 (trade pbk) 1-936092-27-1
Printed in the United States of America

Library of Congress Cataloging-in-Publication Data

Carrier, Michael.
SUPERIOR PERIL / by Michael Carrier. 1st ed.
ISBN: 978-1-936092-27-7 (trade pbk. : alk. paper)
1. Hard Boiled Thriller 2. Mystery 3. Thriller 4. Novel 5. Murder 6. Burglary 7. New York. 8. Michigan's Upper Peninsula.

Contents

What people are saying about the Getting to Know Jack Series.........................10

Author's notes...11

Chapter 1—The bomb..12

Chapter 2—Red's revelation...14

Chapter 3—Kate insists Red texts..17

Chapter 4—The year was 1787 BC..19

Chapter 5—By the Edmund Fitzgerald..22

Chapter 6—Setting sail in 1787 BC...25

Chapter 7—The other two ships set sail...28

Chapter 8—His choice was simple..30

Chapter 9—The Mino has a problem...31

Chapter 10—The Mino goes down..34

Chapter 11—Jack checks with the experts..36

Chapter 12—A day at the museum..40

Chapter 13—What we have here is a failure to communicate...........................44

Chapter 14—The press conference..45

Chapter 15—The Minoan copper ship...48

Chapter 16—Roger the Secret Service man...50

Chapter 17—A new disclosure..54

Chapter 18—Ninth body...57

Chapter 19—Convolution..59

Chapter 20—Camp 33...64

Chapter 21—Robby!..66

Chapter 22—Mom says yes...68

Chapter 23—Flash drive..70

Chapter 24—Jack searches scene for life...73

Chapter 25—Robby, can you hear me?..75

Chapter 26—Jack confronts paramedic...77

Chapter 27—Roger voices concern..80

Chapter 28—Allison—she's back is back...82

Chapter 29—Jack weighs his words...85

Chapter 30—Cadillacs don't float...87

Chapter 31—Advice for Roger...89

Chapter 32—Jack re-encounters 'Sheriff' Green..92

Chapter 33—Sheriff Green questions Jack about Escalade 95

Chapter 34—The men in the Black Jeep..98

Chapter 35—Sheriff silences Jack..100

Chapter 36—No place for leather sandals...102

Chapter 37—From Escalade to Jeep?...104

Chapter 38—Now that's interesting!..107

Chapter 39—Tracking down the Jeep...110

Chapter 40—Kate flirts...112

Chapter 41—The DMC? 114

Chapter 42—A not so funny thing happened..117

Chapter 43—Jack in slow pursuit...119

Chapter 44—Yeah, I'm a cop!...121

Chapter 45—Jack turns his attention to passenger....................................124

Chapter 46—Sorry, gotta go...128

Chapter 47—The excitement never ends...131

Chapter 48—It has Jack going in circles...133

Chapter 49—Jack admits mistake...135

Chapter 50—Proceeding with caution..137

Chapter 51—Jack gets a surprise..139

Chapter 52—Jack searches for Kate...142

Chapter 53—The search for Kate and Robby continues.....................144

Chapter 54—Too many questions, not enough answers.....................146

Chapter 55—Jack questions the paramedic.....................................140

Chapter 56—Jack must find Kate..152

Chapter 57—Jack grills Red..154

Chapter 58—Jack warns Red..157

Chapter 59—Step by step..159

Chapter 60—Red has Jack's back 161

Chapter 61—Detective work can be a nasty job...............................163

Chapter 62—Jack's first real clue...166

Chapter 63—The second clue...168

Chapter 64—The badge talks to Jack..171

Chapter 65—The breakfast..173

Chapter 66—Jack bends the truth...175

Chapter 67—And then there's pain...177

Chapter 68—Kate's plots her escape...179

Chapter 69—These guys are not pros..183

Chapter 70—Kate spots her opportunity...185

Chapter 71—Kate plots to divide and conquer.................................198

Chapter 72—Kate is a cop, after all..190

Chapter 73—Duct tape—man's strength, or his weakness?................193

Chapter 74—Quietman grows more quiet..195

Chapter 75—Blood starved..197

Chapter 76—The sticky pool..200

Chapter 77—It ran like a Ford truck...203

Chapter 78—They've got him!..206

Chapter 79—Setting the trap...209

Chapter 80—Trap set—need cheese..211

Chapter 81—Let the fireworks begin...214

Chapter 82—Jack under arrest?...216

Chapter 83—Sheriff Green checks the GPS.....................................219

Chapter 84—Jack tries to piece story together...............................222

Chapter 85—Roger—in the nick of time...225

Chapter 86—Clear as mud..228

Chapter 87—One mystery solved—they weren't alone..................231

Chapter 88—Meanwhile, back at the hospital................................234

Chapter 89—Sudden impact...238

Chapter 90—Surveying the scene...240

Chapter 91—Make-believe nurse..243

Chapter 92—Jack needs new wheels...247

Chapter 93—No time for Roger..250

Chapter 94—Jack determines the text is bogus..............................252

Chapter 95—Art of setting traps..254

Chapter 96—So far so good...258

Chapter 97—Jack's plan hits a snag...260

Chapter 98—Revision or improvisation?..263

Chapter 99—Surprise surprise...266

Chapter 100—Crash bang boom...268

Chapter 101—Red to the rescue...270

Chapter 102—Story not over...272

Chapter 103—As might be expected...274

Chapter 104—Trouble trouble trouble...277

Chapter 105—The sheriff wants a meeting......................................279

Chapter 106—The man was a doctor..282

Chapter 107—Red explains..285

Chapter 108—Red retraces..287

Chapter 109—Roger completes his thought....................................299

Chapter 110—Major Connections...292

Chapter 111—The pictures...294

Chapter 112—If it shines like gold...296

Chapter 113—Jack: "This has to make sense".............................299

Chapter 114—Dr. Crooked Nose..302

Chapter 115—The sheriff distracted...305

Chapter 116—Crime only half solved...307

Epilogue—going for the gold..309

Cast of Characters of Jack Handler Series....................................312

CasAdditional Comments on Jack Handler Series.......................318

Map..321

The Inscrutable Puzzle?..322

Fascination with the Minoan Newberry Tablet............................324

What people are saying about the "Getting to Know Jack" series

Move over James Patterson and David Baldacci, there's a new author … Michael Carrier is the newest great suspense author!!! Murder on Sugar Island is an intense thrill ride!! Michael Carrier's character Jack Handler is a retired Chicago detective who keeps finding himself in the middle of suspenseful situations…. I seriously couldn't put this book down!!! Definitely a must read for those who enjoy David Baldacci, James Patterson, and Michael Connelly. — Mario

Finally, there is a new author who will challenge the likes of Michael Connelly and David Baldacci. In this latest mystery, Sugar Island (in Michigan's beautiful Upper Peninsula) is used as a fitting backdrop to the wild action. It is a fast-paced thriller that you won't want to put down until the final page. — Island Books

Murder on Sugar Island is a fast-paced mystery full of twists and turns. If you like James Patterson, you'll enjoy Michael Carrier's second novel in the Getting to Know Jack series. This riveting thriller will keep you turning pages all the way to the shocking end. — Cascade Writer's Group

A good read. I thoroughly enjoyed it, and kept coming back to it whenever I had the free time. The characters were really good. Connelly and Baldacci should approve. — Dave

Author's Notes

SUPERIOR PERIL (PERIL) is volume three of the "Getting to Know Jack" series. The first volume of the series is entitled *JACK AND THE NEW YORK DEATH MASK (JACK)*, and the second is *MURDER ON SUGAR ISLAND (SUGAR)*. Both are available in print and eBook (Kindle) formats. Three of the four main characters in *PERIL* (Jack Handler, Kate Handler, and Red) were introduced in the first two volumes. A brief bio of the main characters is available at the end of this book, and on the publisher's website at http://www.greenwichvillageink.com.

If you enjoy this book you should consider writing a short review on Amazon after reading it. (http://amzn.to/1lkMe6i).

If you would like to learn a little more about why you should write an Amazon review, please visit this site: http://www.greenwichvillageink.com/reviews.htm. It will be greatly appreciated.

DISCLAIMER: *SUPERIOR PERIL* is not a true story. It is work of fiction. All characters, names, situations, and occurrences are purely the product of the author's imagination. Any resemblance to actual events, or persons (living or dead), is totally coincidental.

Regarding the credibility of ancient Minoan exploration and exploitation of Michigan's Upper Peninsula—the reader can be the judge.

For additional information visit the publisher's webpage at http://www.greenwichvillageink.com.

The author, Michael Carrier, holds a Master of Arts degree from New York University, and has worked in private security for over two decades.

Chapter 1

The Bomb

(A brief back-story is provided in the "Cast of Characters" section at the end of this book)

How far will this transmitter work? What I mean is, wouldn't it be better to use a cell phone to trigger it? I've heard the terrorists use cell phones. That way they can be somewhere far away, somewhere safe when it blows."

"Didn't we agree—you'd let *me* worry about the explosives, and you'd take care of all the rest of it? You need to back off so I can do my job."

"And I am taking care of my end. But I'm putting my neck on the chopping block right along with you. If this bomb doesn't work right, my career is done."

"If we don't do *anything*, our careers are destroyed anyway. Look, this isn't rocket science. If those two idiots in Boston could build bombs out of pressure cookers and fireworks … that is, *successfully* build bombs, I certainly can make an explosive device that can destroy one car."

"I'm not questioning that. I know you're smart—"

"That's the whole matter. This bomb has to look homemade. If we over design it, with exotic components, it will be easy to trace.

"Look, here's the deal. I want to use materials that anyone can get their hands on—"

"But pressure cookers and fireworks? Come on! Isn't that carrying this *simplicity* thing too far?"

"Not at all. It's easier and safer to buy fireworks, *good* fireworks, than it is to buy plastic explosives. Especially around the holiday. And these particular fireworks are virtually artillery shells. Put enough of this stuff in an enclosed container, and you could blow up a train."

"If you don't pull this off … if this thing doesn't work right … my life is over. I just want it to work right."

"And if we don't do anything? If we just walk away and let matters take their natural course? What then?"

"Same thing. We've been over that a hundred times."

"Then that should make it very simple for you. In a few days, it will all be over and we can get back to business as usual. Isn't that what you really want? To get back to the way it was before?

"So just back off. Working with this crap is nerve-wracking enough without you looking over my shoulder and second-guessing everything. Okay? Just please back off."

Chapter 2

Red's revelation

D id you have fun?" Kate asked Red, as Jack helped him toss his filthy green canvas bag into the back of their SUV.

Jack and his daughter Kate had driven from her Sugar Island resort to pick up Red at the end of his summer camp, which was located near Whitefish Point in Michigan's Upper Peninsula.

Still not able to talk as a result of damage done to his voice box several years earlier, Red smiled at Kate and grunted his affirmation.

Red looked younger than most fourteen-year-old boys. While his physical stature was normal for a boy that age, his ringlets of curls (which Kate described as a tangerine sunset) framed his fine features in such an angelic fashion it caused him to appear more youthful.

Kate had tried to convince him to get a haircut before camp, but Red objected. All those years of living on his own had conditioned him to prefer an unkempt look, so she temporarily acquiesced to his wishes on that issue.

But now that camp was finished, Kate's attention turned to preparing her cousin for school. Her eyes followed him closely as he latched his seatbelt. *Just look at those clothes*, she thought, *I'm glad to see that dirty tee and those crusty jeans. But tomorrow, tomorrow we get your haircut, and then we hit Wal-Mart for school supplies. And some new clothes. That gray hoodie has gotta go.*

Kate could tell by his smile and hug that he was very happy to see her and her dad.

Even though Red could not utter words, he and Kate were learning to communicate. A smile, grunt, and a nod meant yes, while a sober face with a shaking head meant a minor no—pretty standard teenage communication, but with a bit more animation.

If Red frowned, shook his head, and pointed both thumbs down, he was signaling a definite no. And when accompanied with a grunt—an emphatic no with an exclamation point.

This rudimentary system was working for the basics. But when serious conversation was required, Red accomplished that just as most teenagers do—he texted.

"Looks to me like you had a good time," Jack chuckled. "At least judging by the amount of dirt you managed to accumulate on your duffle bag and pillow."

Red looked over and shot a smile at his uncle.

Jack then slid behind the wheel, directly in front of the boy.

"It sure is good to have you back," Kate said, turning around to check out Red's physical condition. "Yeah, I think I would agree with Dad. You must have had a lot of fun. You haven't stopped grinning since you got in the car."

Red just nodded his head yes and continued to smile.

"I know one thing for sure," Kate said. "Buddy sure misses you."

Buddy—a one-year-old golden retriever—was Red's best friend. Red had requested to take Buddy to camp with him. But when informed that dogs were not permitted, Red did not want to go either.

Finally, Jack and Kate convinced him to leave Buddy in the care of Scott and Mary Lundgrun, the cooks and live-in caretakers at the resort Kate owned on Sugar Island.

Both Red and Buddy were totally familiar with those surroundings because it was where they lived year-round.

While Kate had been appointed Red's legal guardian, she did not think he was ready to be uprooted and moved to a big city. So, she opted at least for the short term to have him stay at the resort while she returned to her job in New York.

At first both she and Jack were a little surprised that the county passively granted approval for this arrangement. But the fact was that the local authorities had previously so exhausted themselves in their efforts to place Red in foster care that they were willing to accept any plan that relieved them of this burden.

"Well, tell us about it," she said, pulling out her cell phone and flashing it at Red. "Tell us all about camp."

Chapter 3

Kate insists Red texts

K ate did not want Red to learn sign language. Instead, she wanted him to talk by texting.

Doctors had told her that Red's problem could be repaired with surgery. However, Red was not yet ready to have the operation. She feared that if he began engaging in signing he would forever be satisfied with that mode of communication. So, until he was willing to submit to the surgery, she determined to teach him how to text.

Besides, she felt that texting proficiency would be useful to Red even after he had his voice box repaired.

"Hd grt time," Red texted. "But 1 prblm."

"Oh, really? And what was that?"

"My frnd—hs dad disapprd."

"What do you mean, disappeared?"

"Robby Gordon's dad. hs mom & a cop picked him up."

"Did he get sick? What do you mean by disappeared?"

"Divng in Lake Superior deep. Disapprd."

"Are you sure about that?"

"Yes. Cmp told ystrdy."

"Dad. You're not going to believe this. Red is saying that the father of one of the kids at his camp went missing."

Kate then turned to Red and said, "If I get any of this wrong, stop me. Okay?"

Red acknowledged her request by nodding his head.

"Apparently they were diving in Lake Superior, and—"

Kate then looked at Red and said, "How many of them disappeared? Do you know numbers?"

Red nodded his head yes, and held up nine fingers.

"Nine! Oh my god! Is that right? *Nine* of them went missing?"

Red again nodded his head in agreement.

"That's a *major* big deal, to have nine disappear on the big lake, or anywhere, for that matter. Do you have any idea where they were diving?" Kate asked Red.

Not expecting an answer, she immediately Googled "missing on Lake Superior."

Chapter 4

The year was 1787 BC

It was early in November 1787 BC. By this time, Minoan ships had been sailing up the Ottawa River from the Atlantic Ocean and into Lake Superior for hundreds of years. The stated purpose for the boat traffic was the rich copper deposits found along the Lake Superior shore, particularly in areas now known as the Keweenaw Peninsula and Isle Royale.

While other parts of the world contained copper, only in this area did it appear so plenteously in its pure state. Here the miners had only to melt the copper down and pour it into ingots appropriately sized for shipping.

Much of this Lake Superior copper occurred in large masses

called float copper. Some of the larger chunks of the pure metal weighed several tons. When the pieces were that huge nothing could be done with them—they were just too heavy to remove and transport, and too tough to cut with the tools available to the miners.

But most of the time the pure copper occurred in smaller deposits, and so could easily be crushed out of the rock using heat and water. In fact, often the pieces of float copper were small enough to ship without any work at all, aside from transferring them to a port and loading them on the ships.

Various Native American tribes were employed by the Minoans to mine and move the copper. They would work in this industry throughout the warmer months of the year and then retreat inland during the harsh winters. Notable among those tribes were the Algonquin-speaking peoples, such as the Chippewa and Ojibwa.

The Minoan merchants themselves, while they frequently mixed freely with the Native Americans, were based out of Crete, an island just south of Greece.

From about 2500 to 1200 BC these traders managed both the mining industry in the area as well as the transportation of the copper ingots to Europe. During that period, it is estimated that more than fifty million pounds of copper were removed from this area. For centuries this trade route flourished, possibly beginning as early as 4000 BC.

For the first thousand years or more the Ottawa River, the principal drainage route for Lake Superior, served as the best route to the open seas.

But by 1800 BC the water levels on the Great Lakes had begun to significantly recede. This, in turn, caused the flow of water in the Ottawa River to drop to a level that would not float the maritime traders' boats, thus forcing them to begin seeking an alternate route. Consequently, sometime between 1800 BC and 1500 BC, Lake Superior traffic by means of the Mississippi River began to pick up.

However, in 1787 BC, when this story starts, the captains of the fifty-to-eighty-foot single-tree-mast ships—the kind with one large rectangular sail—still opted for the northern route.

This northern shipping route took the Minoan sailors from Lake Superior into Lake Huron and then on toward the Atlantic through the Ottawa River Basin.

Once they reached the Atlantic Ocean, they skirted along the numerous islands that dot the map of the Northern Atlantic. Those islands were so close together, in fact, that seldom were the ships out of sight of land for longer than a day.

But it was November. And that rich Minoan sailing tradition dictated that it was just about time to shut down operations for the winter.

Chapter 5

By the Edmund Fitzgerald

R ed then texted: "By Edmnd Ftsgrld."

"Really?" Kate said. "The lake is over five hundred feet deep there. That's a mighty big hole to get lost in. Dad, did you hear anything about that?" Kate asked, glancing over at her father. She had not yet been able to access Google.

Kate resembled her late mother more than she did her father. She was thin and tall, and when she was not in her NYPD detective mode, her five-feet-eight-inch, one-hundred-and-twenty-pound frame could have been mistaken for that of a runway model.

Her long chestnut hair fell in large curls around her shoulders. While working she wore it tied back with a black scrunchie, which seemed to set off her green eyes.

Today she was wearing her dark denim skinny jeans, a sleeveless white shirt, and a pair of Steve Madden wedge sandals. They matched her Marc Jacobs satchel.

As her father started to talk she lifted her sunglasses to the top of her head and listened intently to what he had to say.

"Actually, I did read something about it this morning—Online News," Jack responded. "But there was nothing official, at least not at that time. From what I heard there were a total of two craft reported as late checking in. One was a mini-sub, the kind used for exploration, and the other a larger boat, the one that supported the mini-sub.

"And I understand that there were quite a few on board—nine, I think. Names have not been released yet, so I'm not sure if they were all men. From what I read they went down looking for some mysterious Minoan cargo vessel."

"Wait a minute," Kate interrupted, "*Minoan*? How could that be? The Minoans? Weren't they around some time before Alexander the Great? Like *way* before the heyday of Greek culture?"

"Apparently this fellow, who I would suppose is the father of Red's friend, had taken a team of experts out to examine a shipwreck he had discovered earlier. He claimed it to be Minoan or Phoenician. The rap on it was that it was some sort of fraud—a fake find. And this Gordon guy, he wanted to prove that it was genuine."

Kate was just beginning to find service on her iPhone. She clicked off Google and tried Drudge. That was running slow as well, so finally she brought up Yahoo. And there it was: "Nine missing on Lake Superior. They went out to take pictures with some experts, and they haven't come back in yet."

"Does it say anything about the weather?" Jack asked.

"The weather was fine," Kate said. "No storms or winds."

"I sure haven't heard about any bad weather," Jack said, pulling into the Paradise Inn's parking lot.

"What's up?" Kate asked.

Chapter 6

The Mino has a problem

H ave you secured the cargo?" Captain Titiku shouted. "That's a mean northwest, and it's going to get worse— much worse."

"Secure the cargo?" the first mate fired back. "It's copper, for god's sake. Just where do you think it's going to go? We've never had to secure it before."

"We've never sailed this late in the season before," the captain barked.

"The cargo is evenly dispersed. Just like always. Nothing special."

"Well, it's too late now. It is what it is. We should be able to deal with the northwest wind if we pay attention to what we're doing. My biggest worry is what we might run into before we make the calm waters."

By "the calm waters," the captain was referring to what is now known as Whitefish Bay. He knew that once he reached the Bay, the storm would be manageable. The problem was that from Isle Royale, the port from which he had sailed two days earlier, to Whitefish Bay, there were no safe harbors into which he might seek refuge were he to get in trouble.

The captain had not intended to sail so late in the year. In fact, if all had gone as planned, by now his ship would have passed Sugar Island and would probably be well down the Ottawa River. That's what he had hoped for.

But when a hairline crack was discovered in the mast, he knew that he dared not sail until the problem had been properly corrected.

At first he considered a repair. However, the Chippewa workmen convinced him that the crack was too severe for any repair to be effective—especially in the face of the storms he might encounter before he reached his homeport. The sixty-foot oak single-tree mast had to be replaced.

The Chippewa craftsman dressed down a beautiful sixty-foot spruce. It was as straight as an arrow, with no blemishes or knots. They told the captain that it would be a perfect fit for his boat.

And it certainly seemed that they'd be right.

They carefully removed the cracked mast without doing further damage to the ship and successfully fitted it with the replacement.

While the operation went smoothly, it pushed the sailing date back three weeks.

Now, it was the tenth of November. In most instances, it would have been perfectly fine to sail this late in the year and still be able to make it unscathed through the Ottawa River Basin.

But this time there was going to be a problem. Just as in the case of the Edmund Fitzgerald 3,762 years later—on this cold November day in 1787 BC, the winds of November came early.

Chapter 7

The other two ships set sail

C aptain Titiku's ship, the Mino, was part of a group of three Minoan ships that sailed as a convoy. The plan was for the small flotilla to set sail together on or before the twentieth of October. But when Captain Titiku discovered the damaged mast on the Mino, plans changed.

The other two ships postponed departure until the twenty-fifth. That's when they finally decided it would be best to at least get them off Kitchi-Gummi (Lake Superior) before harsh weather set in.

Captain Titiku declared that his friend, Captain Thera of the Kasos, should take his place as leader of the group until he was able to catch up with them.

If all went well, the first two ships would wait for the Mino at the mouth of the Ottawa River, and then the three of them would proceed together on through to the Atlantic Ocean. Captain Titiku told his friend to remain anchored and waiting for no more than three days. If he could not get the Mino to that location by that time, Captain Thera should proceed without him.

The first part of the route carried the two ships from Isle Royale eastward, passing just south of what is now known as Michipicoten Island. Once past the Island, they steered to the southwest, taking them into the calm waters of Whitefish Bay, and then through the rapids of the St. Mary's River.

Aside from the St. Mary's rapids (which now have been replaced by the Soo Locks), the route was almost identical to that used by current freighters carrying iron ore from Duluth to the steel mills in Cleveland.

Once past the rapids, they headed north, seeking out the deeper waters of the Lake George route around Sugar Island on the Canadian side, and then on toward the Ottawa River.

The modern-day shipping lane for that part of the trip has dramatically changed. Toward the end of the nineteenth century AD dredging deepened the St. Mary's channel south of Sugar Island, allowing even the thousand-foot Great Lakes freighters to hug the Michigan shore. This shortened the distance significantly, chopping nearly a full day off the time it takes today's freighter to reach Lake Huron.

Unfortunately, the repair work on the Mino had taken much longer than anticipated. That left Captain Titiku with a very difficult decision: Should he surrender his ship to the frigid Lake Superior winter or take his chances on escaping through to Lake Huron.

Chapter 8

His choice was simple

Neither captain nor crew knew anything about surviving the cold Lake Superior winter, and there was certainly no place to dock the Mino. If he remained there until spring, he and his crew would have to hitch a ride on another ship to get back to his homeport.

Besides, while he understood that the Native Americans migrated away from the lake until spring, he had never ventured far from the port.

So his choice was simple—he would see that the repairs were completed and that the pine pitch tar had sealed the work in a satisfactory fashion, and then he would head out. Even with the potential for bad weather on the horizon.

Chapter 9

The Mino sets sail

At first the crew of the Mino rather enjoyed the boost the stiff northwester provided them. All they had to do was keep the sail set to catch the wind straight on, and it would do all the work.

When they pushed off, the Canadian breeze was not very great—perhaps ten to twelve knots. But as they lost sight of land, it seemed to pick up significantly.

Two hours into their trip, and well out into the lake, gusts began to top twenty knots, with sustained winds of about fifteen knots.

Captain Titiku had many times seen winds much stronger than this on the Atlantic. But when the winds hit gale force, with gusts topping thirty knots, the big lake churned into a frenzy of whitecaps.

And then it started to rain. Because the temperature had fallen, the rain began freezing on the mast and sail. This Captain Titiku had never experienced before.

So the captain gave orders to drop the sail before it ripped apart in the frigid wind. But his crew was unable to lower it due to the heavy buildup of ice. Instead, they turned it so that it did not catch much wind.

However, even without the aid of a sail, the wind carried them along swiftly toward Michipicoten Island.

By daybreak, Captain Titiku determined they had reached the midway point between Isle Royale and Michipicoten Island.

Under most circumstances that would have been good news, especially given the fact that they were not even using their sail. But there were other pressing matters that were captivating the captain.

For one thing, not only had the wind not subsided, but it had gained strength. Now gusts were whistling across the mast at forty knots. And the temperature had steadily dropped. Ice had built up nearly an inch thick on everything exposed.

Furthermore, the rain had switched mostly to snow. This could have been good, had the winds let up. But they did not. With every single swell waves crashed over the side of the Mino. Crew members attempted to bail water, but they could find nothing to stand on that was not covered with ice. Eventually, they simply had to give up and let the storm have its way.

Just before nightfall, they caught sight of Michipicoten Island, and Captain Titiku ordered a ten-degree turn starboard. That, he hoped, would take them toward Whitefish Bay and safety.

At first all seemed well. The Mino's rudder successfully turned the ship in the desired direction. But as it did, the sail caught a near seventy-knot gust, ripping it off the ropes that secured it at the bottom.

Because it had been made heavy and brittle by the frozen rain that had built up on it, when it came back down it crashed into the mast, breaking it off twenty feet up. And then the whole top of the mast and the sail came crashing down on the bow of the Mino, knocking several sailors off the ship and causing severe damage to the hull.

It was now only a matter of time.

Chapter 10

The Mino goes down

There was nothing Captain Titiku could do. While he was headed in the general direction of Whitefish Bay, it was still nearly fifteen miles away. With the help of the rudder and the wind, he knew he was headed in that direction, but he knew that he would never make it.

And so did his crew.

The best they could hope for at this point was to go down together. Even though the boat had not broken up, it continued to take water with every swell. And without a sail, there was no way to keep the bow pointed into the twenty-foot waves.

After what seemed an eternity, a huge wave hit the Mino on the port side. It surprised them all to realize that they were dealing with two seas now—the second one churned up by a front coming in from the northeast.

A second huge wave on the port side pushed the bow well beneath the water—a position from which it could not recover.

Gravity shifted the copper ingots in the hold toward the bow. The rapid change in weight distribution lifted the stern high into the air. The Mino remained vertical for a few seconds, as the copper ingots tumbled into the farthest reaches of the bow. The ship then pierced the surface of Lake Superior like a dagger.

Many of the crew members had earlier crawled under the hull to keep out of the weather. They road the boat 530 feet to the bottom—the cold waters of Lake Superior paralyzing them before they could utter a word to their mates.

Those who had been clinging to the mast were smacked into the frigid waters as the Mino darted downward. They, too, were instantaneously rendered helpless by the lake known never "to give up its dead."

There, in the quiet depths of the largest freshwater lake in the world, they all died within seconds of one another.

Within the week, their flesh had been eaten by fish and other Lake Superior creatures. While their skeletal remains out-survived their soft tissue for hundreds of years, eventually even their bones succumbed to the constant churning of the cold fresh waters.

By 2013 all that remained of the 65-foot Minoan vessel was its basic framework, and it had so yielded to the lake's forces that it stood barely a meter off the floor. Fifty feet starboard lay the fractured single-tree mast, the cross-member that had supported its rectangular sail, and several tons of very corroded copper ingots, along with numerous metal objects large and small.

Chapter 11

Jack checks with the experts

W e're only ten miles from the Shipwreck Museum—the historic Coast Guard station at Whitefish Point," Jack said. "We might as well see what they have to say."

Jack did not apply a conventional approach to investigation. In fact, he loathed tradition. For one thing, he never took notes. It was almost as though he had a heightened sense of smell, like he could tell when someone was lying, or being deceptive in any way. If he was asking a question, and he didn't like the answer, he'd been known to slug a man in the gut, pull his head back with a handful of hair, and say something like this: "You really sure you want to lie to me?"

Of course, he'd have his face inches from the suspect's nose, and he'd be mixing his words liberally with spittle.

As far as Jack was concerned there was no such thing as a "person of interest." To Jack, everyone was a suspect.

He had taken early retirement from the Homicide Division of the Chicago Police Department. He had left the force for a few reasons.

First of all, he hated paperwork. In Jack's mind, that was motivation enough. But he had other reasons.

He had been called up on charges more than any of the other detectives in his precinct. They never stuck well enough to threaten his job, but he had grown very weary of being forced to defend himself and his methods.

But the biggest reason he wanted out was money—he found that he could make much more of it in the private sector.

So, it became a no-brainer—he took an early retirement.

Jack was not a particularly large man: five feet ten inches. For the past ten years he had maintained his weight at one hundred and seventy five pounds.

For a "sixtyish" man, Jack was in incredible condition. He worked out daily regardless of where he was.

Because he was trim, his green eyes and sandy-colored hair gave him a more youthful appearance than his years would have liked to dictate.

He always wore standard cut jeans and a pair of black Asics Gel-Kayano-19 shoes.

If needed, he'd don a black leather jacket over a black pullover. If he wanted a more formal look, he'd ditch the jacket in favor of a linen blazer.

But the blazer was as far as he would go in that direction.

"Great idea," Kate agreed. "I'll try Google again and see what I come up with. Sometimes I get pretty good service from here to the point."

Even in the heat of summer rich green trees frame in breathtaking fashion this eleven-mile stretch from the village of Paradise to Whitefish Point. And every so often, if you're quick enough, it allows a quick peek through the pines at the calm bay waters to the east.

Halfway through a huge set of horse-drawn logging wheels stand like centurions guarding the area's great logging heritage.

A few miles closer to the point is the historic post office, which now serves both as a museum and as a residence for interns employed by the bird sanctuary for migration counting. Opened in the 1870s, the mail was delivered to it by boats during the warm months and by dogsled in the winter.

Just before arriving at the point, the Whitefish Bay State Harbor sign marks the home of the familiar fishing tugs frequently seen throughout the bay and eastern Lake Superior. This Native American industry provides fresh and smoked whitefish to the Upper Peninsula and beyond.

Kate did have better luck the second time. She searched for "recent boat missing on Lake Superior" and found a dozen articles relating to it. She selected the first entry, and read it aloud.

"The Coast Guard reported Thursday that a forty foot cruiser has failed to check in. The boat named 'Snoopy,' with a total of nine on board, left Sault Ste. Marie Thursday morning but never returned.

"According to Captain Gordon's wife, he and his crew had

planned to drop a mini-sub vessel at the location where he had discovered a shipwreck earlier this year. His purpose was to photograph the wreck, which is thought to be located on or near the US/Canadian border, less than a kilometer from the wreck of the Edmund Fitzgerald.

"The shipwreck was reputed by Captain Gordon to be that of an ancient Minoan vessel, which he thought to have sunk sometime before 1200 BC.

"However, most scholars doubted his find.

"The purpose of this mission was to document the shipwreck's authenticity."

Kate stopped reading and looked up.

"He's serious—this Tytus Gordon," Kate said. "He really thought—thinks—that the Minoans sailed into Lake Superior. What would that be, over three thousand years ago? Dad, what do you know about that?"

"Not much. The Minoans were before the Phoenicians. I've read about the Phoenicians quite a bit. They built those beautifully elegant sailing vessels. But I don't think anyone is suggesting that they made it to the Americas."

"I know what I'm going to be Googling when we get back to Sugar Island," Kate said.

"What's that?"

Chapter 12

A day at the museum

S hipwrecks in Lake Superior," Kate replied. "Find out if any ancient ships have ever turned up."

"Might not have to wait that long. I recently met the director of the Shipwreck Museum. He really impressed me. I think he knows the coordinates of virtually every shipwreck on Superior."

"There's a lot of them? Shipwrecks on Superior, I mean?" Kate asked.

"I think there were over five hundred—and many of them occurred not far from Whitefish Point. But I'm not certain as to how many of them were *ancient*."

"Is that where the Edmund Fitzgerald went down?"

"That's right. I think it sunk about sixteen miles off the point."

"Then that's about where this Gordon guy went missing too, at least that's what the report suggests."

"It had to have been if he claims to have found his Minoan shipwreck only a couple thousand feet from Big Fitz."

"Red," Kate said, turning her attention toward the boy. "What else did you hear? Is there anything else?"

Red was half asleep in the backseat. But when he heard his name he sat up and looked at her for a moment. He then began nodding his head yes. He lifted his cell phone and began texting her.

Kate took a closer look at him as he worked his phone. It looked to her as though his hair had grown an inch while at camp. She also observed just how incredibly filthy his clothes were. *Got to introduce those jeans to some Tide*, she thought.

Red lifted his cell to indicate that he had finished texting.

"Robby. Diver's son. Spposed to go out 2 bt came 2 camp instead."

"Oh, how sad. Did he take it hard?"

Red did not text his reply—he simply nodded his head almost to excess, indicating that his friend took it *very* hard. He then signed tears running down his face.

"Text it—don't sign it," Kate said emphatically.

Kate was adamant about how she wanted Red to deal with his inability to talk. She strongly feared that if he became too adept at signing, that he would never have the courage to go through with his reparative surgery. So, every time he tried to use sign language, she would stop him and insist that he text her.

If he had no cell phone available to him, she permitted him

to use pencil and paper. But he was not permitted to sign beyond communicating a yes or a no with head movement.

Red was used to Kate's abruptness regarding his signing, and he did his best to comply.

Red texted: "Robby cried a lot. Couldn't quit."

Kate read his message and smiled at him. "How terribly sad," she said, gently touching his cheek with her left hand. "That must have been hard for you—seeing your friend so hurting."

Kate then addressed her father: "This doesn't make much sense to me. How could a ship that size, with nine on board, just disappear in good weather?"

"These things just don't happen, not today, with radio communication and all. It'll be interesting to hear what the director has to say about it."

"These five hundred shipwrecks in Lake Superior—what seemed to be the biggest cause?"

"From what I understand, there are a few major causes—aside from defective equipment.

"First, weather has played a major factor in many of the shipwrecks. Of course, that could not be the case this time. ... That is if this boat *actually* went down. Certainly, there's nothing we know about right now to indicate that it did go down.

"It's also possible that it could have developed a catastrophic mechanical failure and simply drifted into the bay. If that happened, it should not take long to confirm it.

"One of the other major causes of the wrecks had to do with pilot error. While it was usually weather to blame, that was not always the case.

"Sometimes one ship would simply run into another one, run

aground, or hit a rock."

"Like the Exxon Valdez?" Kate asked.

"Pretty much. But navigation is so much better than it used to be. There actually hasn't been a major shipwreck in Lake Superior since the Edmund Fitzgerald in '75."

"Shouldn't something be floating up if that's what happened?" Kate asked.

"You might think so. But with Big Fitz, all that ever washed up was a beat-up lifeboat. Very strange about Lake Superior—how something as huge as Big Fitz can just disappear without hardly yielding a trace. It's just like that Gordon Lightfoot song."

"What's the other thing?" Kate asked. "You said that there were a few possible reasons the boat didn't come in."

Chapter 13

A failure to communicate

As Jack slowed approaching the Whitefish Point Light Station, he continued: "It's always possible that for some reason they sailed west. It shouldn't be a factor in this case, because there is really a lot of open water west of Whitefish Point, and there are not that many safe harbors. I can't imagine the *Snoopy* intentionally sailing west, unless headed toward Isle Royale, or Keweenaw. But, that would be a third possibility, I suppose, depending on what they had in mind. But, it still wouldn't explain their failure to communicate their intentions. It'll be interesting to see what the Coast Guard has to say."

"What's going on?" Kate interrupted. "Looks like a rock concert."

Chapter 14

The press conference

They had just passed the sign for State Harbor—still almost half a mile from Whitefish Point. Already cars were lined up on both sides of North Whitefish Point Road.

Kate looked around as Jack parked. "They've got media trucks all the way from Traverse City and Grand Rapids. I've not seen so many uplinks since the World Trade Centers came down. They must think the worst has happened."

"Let's get up there. Maybe they're going to hold a press conference."

Kate immediately reached into the backseat and pulled out her Nike AirMax Trainers, while at the same time slipping off her platform sandals. *Platforms are not so good in the sand,* she reasoned as she prepared for a brisk but short trek from the Tahoe to the visitors' observation deck overlooking Lake Superior for what appeared to be a press conference.

All three of them bolted from the SUV and started trotting down the road toward the Light Station. They observed that most of the activity seemed centered out on a deck overlooking the point, just north of the station. From that deck you could see Canada off in the distance.

"Looks like they've set up a podium out there for something—maybe a briefing," Kate observed. "But the crowd hasn't gathered yet. Must be they've announced a time for it."

"Hey, buddy, how long before the conference?" Jack asked a young man assisting a cameraman who was headed toward the deck.

"One hour," he replied. "No crowd yet, but if you've got to set up equipment, you should get to it now."

Jack stopped abruptly. "No need to go out there. Let's see if we can corner the museum manager. It'll be the Coast Guard's show, but the museum manager will know all that's going on."

"Do you know him?"

"I've met him. But I do know Tom Farnquist, the former director of the Great Lakes Shipwreck Historical Society."

"Farnquist," Kate repeated. "He's like a legend. Wasn't he instrumental in recovering the bell from the Edmund Fitzgerald? Isn't that right?"

"That's right. I think we can slide in the museum here and get them to give him a call."

"Hold on," Kate said. "I think that's the museum manager right there, walking this way. At least he looks like the guy on this brochure."

"That's him," Jack said, "follow me."

Larry French was just arriving and appeared to be headed toward his office in the museum.

"Larry," Jack boomed. "Jack Handler. Remember me? Chicago homicide, retired. We met earlier this year. I was with Tom Farnquist."

"Yes, of course. How are you?"

"Our young man here is very concerned about his friend's father—Tytus Gordon. He was on that boat exploring a shipwreck out by the Fitzgerald. Do you have any further info on that?"

"The Coast Guard, Captain Mark Elliot to be specific, is holding a press conference in about fifty minutes. You're welcome to hear what he has to say."

"Any plans on running the Boyd out there?"

The *R. V. David Boyd* is a forty-seven-foot survey vessel. It carries on it a Phantom S4 remotely operated exploratory vessel capable of diving to the deepest parts of Lake Superior.

"Not my call," the manager replied. "The Captain has suggested that possibility, but nothing has been settled yet."

"Still no word from the missing boat?"

"None. We've got some boats out there looking for oil or debris—some of ours and some private. But so far we've found nothing."

"You do know where they were and what they were doing, right?" Jack asked.

Chapter 15

The Minoan copper ship

"We do. They were taking a look at the bottom, getting some pictures of the shipwreck everyone's been talking about. That supposed Minoan copper ship."

"Then your people haven't checked it out?"

"We've talked about it, but those things cost money. The board has to vote on something like that. Besides, there's some question as to whether it's on our side or the Canadian."

"So, does that mean that the only evidence so far of that ship are the images shot by Tytus Gordon?"

"That's true. And so far the experts have not authenticated the find. That's what their trip was all about—authentication. Say, Jack, it was nice to see you again, but I've got to go. It's a busy place around here right now. You are welcome to stay and catch the press conference and even ask the Captain some questions. Follow me into the museum, and I'll get you a pass."

"Thanks, but I think you've answered my questions. It was good to see you as well, and I hope this all turns out for the best."

"Be praying," the manager said as he turned to walk away.

"Wow," Kate said, "that doesn't sound very promising."

"No, it doesn't," Jack replied. "I've got an idea. If I've got any cell coverage here, I'm going to see what my buddy in DC knows about this."

Seeing he had two bars on his cell, he dialed Roger, his friend in the Secret Service.

"Roger. Jack here. I'm fine … except I've got a favor to ask … again. What can you find out about—"

Chapter 16

Roger the Secret Service man

Y ou don't even have to say it," Roger Minsk said. "You want to know what I can find out about this Gordon fellow, and the *Snoopy*. Am I right?"

Jack and Roger had been friends for decades. Roger had made the rounds in his work with the Secret Service. In the early nineties he had been attached to the White House—specifically to protect the president. That's when Jack first met him.

Later he was handpicked by a former first lady for her detail. Roger had a reputation for doing a first-rate job as well as knowing how and when to back off and allow those he protected some privacy.

Currently Roger remained assigned to the former first lady's detail.

But Roger's reputation extended well beyond his willingness to take a bullet for the one he was assigned to protect.

It was thought by many in the know that Roger had more connections than the directors of the CIA and FBI. In fact, the former president and the former first lady feared Roger in much the same way as everyone in DC had feared J. Edgar Hoover. Roger had just the right amount of dirt on everyone.

"My cell indicated where I was calling from, and you figured it out from there. But you're absolutely right—that's why I'm calling. You always seem to know more than anyone else."

"Not that so much—I just always share more with you than I should."

"Probably true," Jack chuckled. "But, about this Tytus Gordon— do you have anything on him that might prove interesting?"

"He's got a reputation as a bit of a wild hare if you know what I mean. Tends to operate on the fringes. I'll do some checking for you. But right off the top, he strikes me as a bit of an Indiana Jones, but without scruples. That might be a bit harsh, but that's my first impression."

"Really?"

"What's your interest?"

"My … my daughter, Kate, has become the significant adult in my nephew's life. He's the kid we rescued last year. You remember? You were instrumental in that effort as well."

"Sure, I remember. I remember that you *still* haven't filled me in on all the outrageous details of that episode. As I recall, you got me involved in clandestine border crossings, the crash of a helicopter, which you had stolen earlier. Bombings in the US and Canada, and, who knows how many killings. My friends are still buzzing about the bombings."

"Sometimes, Rog, the less you know, the better off you are. I sure hope this conversation doesn't end up on some computer in Ft. Meade."

"It can't. This network is the same one the presidents use. It even secures *your* phone, provided you call me on a cell. Just be aware that all bets are off when you use a landline."

"That's nice to know," Jack said. But he already knew that when he talked to Roger, both ends of the conversation were digitally reconstituted, making the recording of them impossible without the right software. And Jack also knew that if a simple recording device were to be installed at his house on a land line, any calls made using that line would not be protected.

"But you got the kid out okay?" Roger said.

"Thanks to you, yes we did."

"Then, I suppose you're thinking that since I helped you save the kid, that somehow I'm now responsible for him. Just pulling your leg a bit. I'm always happy to help you. You get yourself into more crap than our favorite former president on a bad day. But, you do help keep my life interesting. Besides, you and I both know that I will be calling in your card someday. And you know what that could mean."

"Anytime. I'm here for you anytime you need my help."

"And knowing that helps me sleep some nights. Never know when I might need some of those very special tools you bring to the table. So, what can I help you with today?"

"If you could just do some snooping around. I'm a bit at a loss for connections up here. If I were back in Chicago, I would be a little more comfortable twisting arms. But up here, I'm just another retired cop."

"Tell me, what's this kid of yours got to do with this missing boat, or whatever it is?"

"Red is friends with the Captain's son—this Gordon guy. And I promised him I'd see what I can do to get to the bottom of it."

"Fair enough."

"It's not life and death for anyone you know or love, at least not yet?"

"That's right."

"But I know you. Once you get started on this, you're going to see it through."

"Kate and I are both intrigued."

"So, Kate is up there with you?"

"Right."

"Okay, I get the picture. You and she are going to solve this mystery. And you don't have much time because she has to get back to work. Is that about it?"

"You nailed it old buddy."

"Oh my god, Handler. I'm just getting something … hang on a second."

Chapter 17

A new disclosure

noopy's been found! You can't talk about this yet. The details aren't being released. But this is what I'm reading: 'The *Snoopy*, a forty-foot cruiser was found run aground at the west end of Little Lake Harbor, about twenty miles west of White-fish Point. The boat had been missing for over twenty-four hours.'

"Now get this. Eight bodies were found on board—cause, or causes of death, have yet to be determined. At least not released."

"Eight?" Jack questioned. "I'd heard there were nine."

"This is an official communiqué I have in front of me. It's from the Department of Homeland Security. It clearly states that eight bodies were found."

"What would Homeland Security be doing with this—shouldn't it be a matter for the FBI?"

"I'm sure that the FBI will soon get involved … if they haven't already. But the initial incident was discovered or preliminarily investigated by DHS. And this report was apparently initiated by them."

"Do you have a list?"

"List of names?"

"Right."

"No. No names. With one exception. Tytus Gordon was listed as among the dead. Must have been they were able to do a positive identification on his body. Let's see, in total, there were the bodies of six men and two women found on the boat."

"Women? I hadn't heard anything about there being women on the boat," Jack said. "When do you think the whole list of names will be available?"

"It won't be released to the public until all identities are confirmed and next of kin notified. I won't even have anything further until the bodies have been positively identified. And it could be some time before that happens."

"Why's that?"

"The boat was scuttled."

"Scuttled! Well, thanks a lot for that suspense," Jack quipped sarcastically.

"Sorry, Jack. That's the DHS for you. They tacked that little detail on the end like it didn't matter."

"What exactly do you mean by scuttled? Was it *intentionally* sunk?"

"Appears that someone ran the boat all the way around the

pier and then crashed it into the T-shaped section of pier from the northeast."

Are you suggesting that this was an *accident*?" Jack asked.

"Hardly! Once they plowed into the steel undergirding, they pulled the plug, and set it on fire. The fire not only destroyed the *Snoopy*, but it destroyed a whole section of the pier. It burned the planks right off it."

"Right there in the harbor," Jack said. "Must be the killer was already on board. That he basically hijacked the boat, killed everyone else, brought it into the harbor, crashed it, set it afire. And then pulled the plug, as you put it. Do you suppose he had a car parked there, or maybe had an accomplice waiting for him?"

"And there's one more thing that you will find interesting. Maybe a bit more than interesting."

Roger then paused for a few seconds. Jack was growing impatient.

Finally, Jack blurted out: "Okay, buddy, you going to tell me, or make me beg?"

Chapter 18

Ninth body

Hang on. There's a new communication just coming in," Roger finally said. "The body of a man was found in a car parked alongside the road, less than a mile from the harbor. He had been shot twice, and the car set afire.

"I suppose a logical assumption would be that this body was somehow connected with the bodies on the boat—maybe the ninth person. There's nothing in this communiqué to suggest that, but I'm sure the FBI will be looking in that direction.

"Holy cow, Jack, everywhere you go it seems people die. What is it about you?"

"Hey. I had nothing to do with that. Who's in charge of this? Must be the FBI, wouldn't you think?"

"Who else? Has to be. Maybe not this minute, but within hours, they'll be arriving like gangbusters."

"Would you stay on top of this and keep me informed? I'm going to head up that way right now and see if I can poke my nose in before the FBI takes over."

"Sure, I'll follow it," Roger replied. "But I don't think you'll have much luck, even this early on. This is already a really big deal."

"Can't hurt to try. Never know who I might run into. Anything at all on that ninth body? The one that was located in the burned-out car?"

"Actually, that body has now been identified," Roger replied. "It is being reported that it belongs to this name: Carl Raymond Jenkins."

"And any info on Mr. Jenkins?"

"Let's see. Mr. Carl Raymond Jenkins ... if it's the same one ... and I'm pretty sure he is the same one ... hails from ... from the Detroit area. But he's resided in the Upper Peninsula for the past twelve years. Most recently he has listed Sault Ste. Marie as his mailing address. Single. Divorced, actually. Only a minor rap sheet. Failure to pay child support, DUI. Nothing violent. No felony convictions."

"What sort of work does he do?"

"He's done carpentry work, off and on. For the past two years he has been on disability—looks like permanent disability."

"What, exactly, does that mean?"

"Can't tell from what I can pull up. But this doesn't look right. See what you think."

Chapter 19

Convolution

Mr. Carl Raymond Jenkins has been drawing government disability checks for the past two years. But, over the last six months his checking account indicates that he has been depositing an additional $500 a week, always in cash."

"Really, that doesn't sound right—cash? Where'd he get that? I wonder if he's paying taxes on it?"

The sound of that single word, "taxes," even coming from his own mouth, caused Jack's mind to wander into unwanted territory. It reminded him of his problems stemming from his purchase of half-interest in a bar in Chicago nearly two decades ago. His partner was one of his oldest and most-trusted friends. The principal reason for his making the investment was not profit. He simply wanted to create a cover for his private security business.

Many, if not most, of his clients insisted on paying him in cash, or with some other untraceable commodity. At first he tried getting rid of the cash by paying all his bills with it. But even though he meticulously avoided credit cards and checks, the cash continued to accumulate.

It wasn't that he was in any manner averse to paying his fair share of taxes. The problem was that if he did deposit the cash into a checking account, and subsequently included it in his filings, he would then at some point be required to explain where it came from.

He needed to find an acceptable method of laundering, and his buddy's bar seemed perfect.

But it did not work out as planned. Almost exactly one year ago the IRS decided to audit the bar.

Jack hired one of his old customers, a disbarred attorney/CPA, to see if this shady character could get the books straightened around enough for Jack to survive the audit and avoid federal prison.

The accountant knew exactly how Jack earned his money and that the sale of a few bottles of Jack Daniels had little to do with it.

Even though his buddy and the CPA talked a good game about establishing legitimacy, Jack still agonized about it when such thoughts barged through his mind.

"Good question. That's not all. If he's paying his child support, his checking account does not reflect it. Sounds like this fellow has a few irons in the fire."

"I'd say he had more than that in the fire," Jack said. "In fact, this whole thing is beginning to sound pretty convoluted. I would probably do well to just keep my nose out."

"Perhaps. Especially if you don't actually have a vested interest. Anyway, it was good to talk to you. And I will keep my eyes open should anything else come across my desk regarding the case. I would really be interested in learning the cause of death, in the case of the eight others."

"I will find out. And it was good to talk to you as well."

Jack knew that Kate had been listening intently to his side of the conversation. He replayed it in his mind, to determine if there were details that he should provide her to fill her in on Roger's side of the conversation. Jack did not want to paint too graphic a picture for Red to hear.

"Did you get the gist of that?" he asked Kate.

"Sure did," she said. "Just how involved do you think we should become?"

"This could really be nasty," he said.

"Could be? I'd say it already was nasty. There can't be any upside here. At least not from what I just heard. Who're the good guys? And who're the bad ones? Any idea?"

"Yeah, I know who the good guys are … and I'm just about to buy them lunch. Beyond that, I haven't a clue."

"Now that sounds good to me," Kate said. "What do you have to say about that?" Kate said, turning back to look Red in the eyes.

Noting that Red's face exhibited extreme concern, she said, "Hey, Red, don't worry about this. Your friend Robby and his mother are fine. I'm sure you figured it out that his father has passed away. Jack and I are really sorry about that. Maybe, after you get settled in at the resort, we can invite Robby to spend a few days with us. You can take him fishing and hiking. I'm sure he would like that. And the distraction would really be good for him. What do you think? Sound fun?"

Red nodded his head, confirming his desire to have his friend over.

"And," Kate continued, "you're probably also aware that it's possible that your friend does not yet know that his father is dead. You must not share any of this information with anyone, particularly with Robby. For now it has to be our secret."

Again, Red indicated he understood and would not pass that information along.

Jack carefully pondered what could be gained by driving out to Little Lake Harbor, the scene of the nine murders. Roger had already filled him in on more of the details than he could possibly garner at the actual site. And while he did trust his own deductive acumen more than that of local law enforcement, he knew that very soon the FBI would be on scene and in charge. Besides, he sensed that Red was hurting for his friend.

"How about lunch at the Upper Tahquamenon Falls?" he enthusiastically suggested.

"Perfect!" Kate said. "Red, you remember eating there before, right? You loved their burgers."

Red acknowledged her question with a two-thumbs-up and then settled back in his seat with a smile on his face, albeit a contemplative one.

Ever since Jack and Kate first started coming to the Upper Peninsula (after she became owner of the Sugar Island Resort), they would always stop at the Upper Falls restaurant if they found themselves in the general area at dinnertime. And they were not alone. The restaurant/pub at the falls had not only become a favorite among tourists, Paradise locals viewed it favorably whenever the Brown Fisheries Fish House ran out of its specialty.

The whole Tahquamenon River basin has a rich history. First made famous by the Longfellow poem Hiawatha, it later became instrumental for the logging industry in the late nineteenth century and well into the twentieth.

Chapter 20

Camp 33

During that period, a logging camp, Camp 33, was constructed at the site of the Upper Falls. A fortune was spent to smooth out the rapids along the river to accommodate its use to transport logs by floating them down the river.

The Upper Falls stands as the second largest waterfall east of the Mississippi River with over fifty thousand gallons of amber-colored water flowing over it every second—the amber color resulting from leaching tannic acid from the cedar and hemlock swamps upstream.

Up until the early 1950s, the falls themselves were inaccessible except by canoe. It was at that time that Jack and Mimi Barrett, grandparents of the current owners, purchased the property adjacent to the falls. Later they built a replica of logging Camp 33 and deeded access to the falls to the State of Michigan to be used as a state park, with the stipulation that only a walk path be constructed back to the falls. Another requirement the owners made was that they be allowed to operate a brewery and restaurant inside the park.

So, when visitors wished to eat or drink beer at the facility, they first had to obtain entry into the state park. But that extra requirement didn't seem to hurt business—the restaurant and pub were almost always full. Jack and Kate favored the whitefish entre, while Red had never ventured beyond the bison burger.

When they reached the intersection of Whitefish Point Drive and the western branch of M-123—the part that passes by Tahquamenon Falls—Kate spotted a car turning west in front of them. She immediately recognized the vehicle as having been at the camp when she initially dropped Red off.

"Red," she said, pointing at the car. "Isn't that one of your friends? In fact, isn't that Robby?"

Chapter 21

Robby!

Red had a huge smile on his face.

"Could it be?" Jack suggested. "Could they be headed to the same restaurant?"

"Isn't that the road to Little Lake Harbor as well?" Kate posed.

"It leads in that direction," Jack agreed. "But I doubt that the news has broken yet. You know, it's possible they are simply going for a burger, just like us. Even in difficult times people still need to eat."

"That could get tricky," Kate said. "Red, whatever you do, don't let on that you know *anything* about Robby's father. Can you handle that?"

Red smiled and began to text.

Kate glanced down at his incoming message: "I promise. Won't SAY a word!"

Kate shot a smile back at him: "Look, smarty-pants. You know what I mean, and why I'm asking you not to communicate with your friend. When the news breaks about his father, he needs to hear it from his mother. I know you get it."

Red smiled again and nodded his head in the affirmative. He was, however, still smiling—as was Kate.

"Hey," Jack said. "Do you know your friend's cell number?"

Again Red signaled yes.

"Great. Why don't you text him to see if they can meet us at the restaurant—I'm buying."

Red and Kate thought that was a great idea.

"Cell service is a little sporadic out here," Kate said. "Robby might not even have his cell on."

Only a few moments passed before Red's phone signaled an incoming text message.

Chapter 22

Mom says yes

R ed viewed his message—it was from Robby. He tapped Kate on the shoulder and let her read it:

"Upper Taq restrant—Mom says yes."

"That's great," Kate said, turning to look at the car ahead. Red's friend Robby had moved into the backseat of his mom's SUV and was waving excitedly out the window.

"He's pretty excited to see you," Jack quipped. "I'll bet you two are just a couple of Tom Sawyers when you get together."

At that moment, all three of the occupants of Jack's vehicle were smiling broadly. They knew that the saddest of news awaited Robby and his mom, but for right now, two fourteen year-old boys were very excited. During those few moments, both Jack and Kate sensed a spirit of frivolity and unity envelope both vehicles. That was going to change dramatically.

Jack was by nature a careful driver. Even though he got a kick out of watching Red and Robby exchange their silly gesticulations, he knew that it would not be safe to follow too closely. The stretch of M-123 running between Paradise and the Tahquamenon State Park, while not treacherous, was at least challenging, due to the way it wound its way around low areas. No sooner did one curve end than another began.

Jack had driven through the area dozens of times—maybe more. Even though he had never seen a moose plodding through the numerous ponds, he still always thought about it. *If hitting a deer could destroy a car*, he reasoned, *smacking into a bull moose would destroy both car and driver.*

So Jack let off on the accelerator, dropping behind the still jubilantly expressive boy ahead of him and avoiding the equally exuberant antics of the one in his backseat.

Then it happened.

Chapter 23

Flash drive

R ed had just received a second text from his friend, and he tapped Kate on the arm to show it to her. Kate turned to read Red's cell when Jack locked his brakes.

The rapid deceleration caught Kate by surprise, and she screamed. Red, who had loosened his seatbelt slightly so that he could more easily be seen by his friend, crashed with force into the back of Kate's seat.

"Oh my god!" Jack yelled in shock, as pieces of Robby's car began to rain down on them. "Their car just blew up!"

Jack immediately checked his rearview mirror to be sure that he would not be rear-ended as he pulled off the road. While there was a car that had been following close behind, Jack was satisfied that it was safe to continue slowing.

"What happened!" Kate shouted.

"Their car just blew up," Jack replied in disbelief.

By that time Jack had fully stopped his vehicle and maneuvered it off the road, exercising care not to run over any debris. He then backed up to avoid the flames and engaged his four-ways.

Jack immediately grabbed his cell and called county dispatch.

"Chippewa County Sheriff Dispatch, how may I help you?"

"My name is Jack Handler. There's been an explosion. The car in front of me. About three miles west of Paradise on M-123. That's the leg of M-123 that heads toward Newberry. Need an ambulance … and a fire truck. I think there were two people in the vehicle—a boy and an adult female."

"Then there are injuries?"

"Definitely."

Kate did not hesitate. She jumped out of the vehicle and joined Red in the backseat and threw her arms around him. He was horror-struck.

Even though Jack did not hold much hope that either of the two occupants could have survived the explosion, he got out to investigate.

The first thing that he observed was a woman's bloody hand and forearm, savagely severed by the explosion—it was lying only a few feet in front of Jack's vehicle.

A large plume of white smoke rose into the air over the explosion told Jack that the explosive device was of rudimentary design— quite possibly constructed of black powder or fireworks packed tightly inside of a constrictive device, similar to what was used in the Boston Marathon bombing.

Not terribly sophisticated, Jack surmised. *But highly effective if placed close enough to the target.*

Generally bombs such as this are used to propel shrapnel, such as nails or BBs. If the IED (improvised explosive device) is placed close enough to the victim, it can blow a person's body into oblivion. But generally the real damage is done by nails, or other small objects placed tightly around the device. When the explosion occurs, those objects are propelled at a high rate of speed.

Jack marveled that there did not seem to be evidence of such shrapnel. He wondered about that. *Could be the bomber used materials that were easy to get, and hard to trace. The purpose was to kill the driver and probably the passenger, but limit collateral damage. He didn't consider the possibility that Robby would have climbed into the far back of the vehicle. That's all that could have saved the boy—his relative distance from the explosion.*

Jack, returning to his vehicle to address his passengers, opened the rear door and looked into Kate's eyes: "Under no circumstance should Red get out of the car. And you should stay and comfort him. This is horrendous. I'm going to see if I can locate the boy."

Kate had cradled Red in her arms and was holding his head to her chest. She did not verbally respond to her father, but she did nod her head.

Jack, hearing tires squeal, turned to see the car that had been following closely behind him rapidly speeding off back toward Paradise.

"Strange," he thought, "that they did not stop and offer assistance." While the car was too far away for him to get a license number, he did recall from earlier that the vehicle was a late-model black Escalade and that there were at least two occupants.

Chapter 24

Jack searches scene for life

Jack knew that there was nothing he could do to help Robby's mother, given that the explosion appeared to have centered near the front of the vehicle. He did, however, want to locate the boy—or the boy's body.

"Robby," Jack shouted. "Son, can you hear me?"

Robby could not hear Jack, but not because he was dead. Both of the boy's eardrums had been damaged by the explosion.

But Jack did not give up. He recalled that just before he dropped back, he was still able to see Robby making faces and waving at Red. He reasoned that with the explosive device located under the driver's seat, which appeared to have been the case, the boy could have survived. So he kept looking.

Finally, after what must have been several minutes, Jack heard moaning coming from the north side of the road. He waded out into the nearly knee-deep ponds that covered the terrain on both sides of the road.

"Robby, do you hear me!" Jack shouted.

Again, the boy didn't answer. But Jack did get a better idea of the boy's location.

"Robby!"

Jack stopped and waited.

"Help," Robby moaned, not far from where Jack was standing. Actually, it seemed to him that the sounds were emanating from an area between him and the site of the explosion. Not far, in fact, from where Jack had just walked.

"Help."

This time Jack got a good fix on the boy's location and headed toward it.

After a few steps, he again stopped and waited.

But this time he spotted the boy before he made another sound. Robby was lying only half a dozen steps from where Jack had just walked.

Chapter 25

Robby, can you hear me?

Dropping to his knees, Jack knelt beside the boy.

"Robby, can you hear me?"

The boy's shirt and shoes had been ripped off by the explosion or by the subsequent flames. The pink and black marks on his bare skin told Jack that the boy had suffered severe burns. Fortunately, the murky waters that now cradled him had extinguished the flames that clearly had accompanied him on his airborne journey.

Carefully Jack examined the boy looking for life-threatening injuries.

Robby's eyes darted back and forth like those of a frightened animal, but he was fully awake and able to move his arms and legs in a controlled fashion.

When the boy tried to stand to his feet, Jack did not discourage him. He wanted to get a better look at his torso.

Aside from some third-degree burns, there did not appear to be any other injuries. At least, no open wounds.

"I can't hear very well," he said. "My head *really* hurts."

Jack was encouraged. "Can you hear me at all?" he asked.

"Yes, but not good."

Making sure that the boy could see his lips, Jack nearly shouted: "Aside from your head, where else do you hurt?"

Robby did not say anything at first. Finally, he held both palms over the burns on his stomach but did not touch them.

"Here, and on my back. It burns."

"Can you walk?"

Robby did not answer. He did take Jack's hand, and the two of them began walking toward Jack's SUV.

Jack laid his jacket on the ground beside his vehicle and told Robby to lie down on it.

Kate, fully aware that the boy was in shock, grabbed Red's sleeping bag and jumped out of the vehicle.

Unzipping it fully, she spread it out over the boy.

Immediately he tried to get up.

"Mom! Where's my mom?"

Chapter 26

Jack confronts paramedic

L ie down, Robby," Kate commanded. "You need to lie down until the paramedics get here. Dad and I will look after your mother."

Within seconds, an ambulance arrived.

Jack ran over to intercept the driver.

"There were two occupants," Jack said.

But the driver did not want to listen. Instead, he snarled and tried to push Jack aside.

Jack grabbed him and slammed him against his ambulance before he could reach the rear of it.

"Who the hell are you?" The driver yelled.

"I'm your worst nightmare if you don't take a moment to listen to me! Got it?"

"You're interfering—"

"Shut up and listen. There were two occupants, a fourteen-year-old boy and his mother. There are parts of her strewn all around here. Safe to say she didn't make it. But the boy is alert. He's around on the side of my vehicle. Be careful what you say to him. He does not know his mother is dead. I'm sure you recognize shock when you see it."

Jack then straightened the paramedic's clothes and commanded: "Now, chief, go do your job."

"You're gonna hear about this, I can promise you that."

"I'm sure I will. Now you do what I said. You go do your job. And you'd better do it very well—I'm gonna be watching you."

Jack took a couple deep breaths, trying to calm down. He then walked around to where Kate waited with Robby.

"They're gonna be taking over here," he said to Kate. "Time for you to get back in the car with Red. He's gonna be needing some attention."

Kate slid into the backseat with Red, and Jack got in behind the wheel.

"I need to get this out of the way. I'm surprised that the ambulance made it here before the sheriff. I'll bet all of their cars are tied up with that missing boat."

"Where're we headed?" Kate asked. "Shouldn't we wait for the sheriff?"

"We should. But that paramedic needs to spend all his energy with Robby. If I stick around, he's gonna be concentrating on me."

"What'd you do to him?"

"Not much, really. I just got his attention. Besides, there was an

Escalade following us, and he seemed in a big hurry to get outta here when the car blew up. They're gonna be sedating the boy now We'll check in later. But for now, we'd just get in the way.

"I really want to see if we can pick up on that Escalade."

And then, just as Jack managed to get his vehicle headed east, his phone vibrated.

"Roger—funny you should call."

Chapter 27

Roger voices concern

"Why do you say that?" Roger asked.

"Fifteen minutes ago—*fourteen* minutes ago—the wife and son of one of the boating murder victims, the captain of the boat, Tytus Gordon, were blown up right in front of me. Red, my nephew, was texting the kid when it happened. Their car exploded, no more than seventy feet away. I think the device was triggered by a black Escalade that was following behind us."

Jack saw that Kate was calling in the Escalade.

"Rog, hang on for just a second," he said.

He then turned his attention to Kate. "Tell them it was a black Escalade. Tinted glass. Michigan plates, but I didn't get a number. Two men, at least. Looked large—well dressed, but can't be sure. It was headed back toward Paradise on M-123. They've got a fifteen-minute jump on us."

Jack then responded to Roger's call: "As you probably figured out, we're in pursuit of the vehicle that I think triggered the device—it was a black Escalade, right behind us. When we stopped, it stopped and turned back east. Something like that is best activated by some sort of RF transmitter. But that's not what you called me about. What's on your mind?"

"Were both killed—mother and son?"

"No. Just the mother. I think the boy will make it."

"That's good," Roger replied. "Two things you should know. Are you sure you can talk now?"

"Sure, fire away."

"First of all, the boat that was sunk is owned by a company called Aqua Maritime, based out of Sault Ste. Marie. The president is a man named Jason Brinks. From what I can see, he has liquidated most of his holdings, and he appears near foreclosure on two properties that he has been unable to unload."

"So, there might be some financial issues going on beneath the surface. Is that how you see it?"

"I'm just saying that the owner of the boat is having problems," Roger replied. "might mean nothing."

"And there was something else?"

Chapter 28

Allison–she's back

Right," Roger said. "But this has nothing to do with your current situation. I just thought you should know. Maybe you already do know. Allison is pushing for the exhumation of Reg's body. Did you know about that?"

"I had heard something. Pam called me a few months ago and told me about it. But I thought that she had put a stop to it. Are you suggesting the exhumation is moving forward?"

"Seems so. I'm not sure what sort of pressures they are bringing to bear on Pam, but it would not be good for any of us if they were to dig Reg up. Do you think you could give her a call and see what you can do? Perhaps after this dust settles a bit?"

A little over a year earlier Jack had been asked by his good friend, Reginald Black, to help him on a job for which he had been contracted. One of Reg's other associates, Former First Lady Allison Fulbright, along with four others, had plotted the assassination of the sitting president. Reg accepted the offer to participate only so that he could thwart it. Because Reg and Jack were the closest of friends, and because Jack had worked with Reg on other jobs, Jack agreed to help Reg prevent the assassination.

As compensation for his effort, Reg promised to pay Jack $10 million in gold. While that would have been Jack's biggest payday of his career, he never collected. Unfortunately, Reg was shot by a rogue group of Eastern European agents. Reg and Jack had stormed the row house in Brooklyn where the agents were holding Kate hostage. The Eastern Europeans had hoped to use Kate to influence Jack's role in the plot.

While Jack and Reg were successful in freeing Kate, Reg was shot.

At the time, Roger had been appointed to head up the Secret Service detail charged with protecting Allison. Once he became aware of the assassination plot, he joined forces with Jack and Reg to actively participate in the effort to undermine it.

Allison, who was ostensibly the mastermind in the conspiracy, never knew that Reg, Jack, and Roger were working against her.

Not only was Allison thoroughly disappointed that the assassination attempt fell through, she was even more angry because she had paid Reg $100 million dollars in gold to facilitate it.

After the shooting at the Brooklyn row house, Roger saw to it that Reg was buried at Calvary Cemetery, just across the East River from Manhattan. He fudged Reg's autopsy to show that he had died from a massive heart attack.

Now Allison wanted to exhume the body. Neither Roger nor Jack wanted to see that happen.

"Yeah," Jack said. "I'll give Pam a call. I'll give Allison a call too if you think it might help."

Chapter 29

Jack weighs his words

I'll call her tomorrow. I'll see what I can find out. My guess is that Allison has bribed Pam. It wouldn't take much. I'm sure that she's not rolling in money. Too bad Reg never freed up any of that gold he received from Allison."

Jack had to be careful what he said in front of Kate. While she knew some things about the conspiracy, Jack made it a point not to discuss any details that could jeopardize Kate's position with the City of New York.

"You never got paid?" Roger asked.

"That's right," Jack said. "At the time, my biggest interest was in saving Kate. And then when Reg got shot, it really didn't seem important anymore."

"Allison wants her money back," Roger said. "I'm sure that's what's prompting this whole thing. Just trust me on this one, Jack. It'd be best for all of us if she could be convinced to back off and leave this whole matter alone."

"Not gonna happen," Jack said. "She's just about as greedy as they come."

"Shame no one knows where all that gold is. I suspect that if Allison were to get her hands on it, she'd be willing to let go of this exhumation business. Anyway, how you doing with your Escalade?"

"No way to know which way he turned at the light in Paradise. I assumed that he would turn south, but I have no way of knowing. I suppose I should wait here for the sheriff. Hey, Rog, I'll talk to you later."

Jack assumed that the Cadillac had turned south in Paradise. He reasoned that if a person were attempting to elude capture, a south turn on M-123 would provide the most options—Newberry, Trout Lake, Brimley, and even the Soo were accessible from that route.

But heading north would leave no way for escape.

However, the driver of the Escalade had something different in mind—he did turn north on Whitefish Point Road. Within ten minutes, the driver and the passenger were at the State Harbor, less than a mile from Whitefish Point.

There they lowered the windows to expedite sinking, and rolled the stolen $60,000 Cadillac SUV off the boat launch into the deep harbor waters.

Chapter 30

Cadillacs don't float

The driver and passenger who had arrived only moments ago in the Cadillac did not wait to confirm the outcome. They simply turned and jumped into the backseat of a black Jeep that had pulled into the State Harbor behind them.

By the time the four occupants of the Jeep reached and turned south on Whitefish Point Road, the Escalade had floated a hundred feet off the ramp and was disappearing beneath the surface.

The weight of the engine pushed the front deeper into the water.

For a few moments, the air that was trapped in the area above the windows and in the rear of the vehicle slowed its descent.

Finally, with an explosion of bubbles, the Escalade dropped beneath the surface. It was virtually invisible once it settled on the bottom.

* * *

"Dad," Kate said with surprise in her voice, "this is really interesting. Captain Spencer has just emailed me. Internal Affairs wants to talk to me about Reginald Black. What do you suppose that's all about?"

Chapter 31

Advice for Roger

Y ou got the gist of my conversation with Roger?" Jack asked.
"Sort of. I heard you say that someone wanted to exhume Reg's body. Do you know who might be behind that? And what that could have to do with IA wanting to rattle my cage?"

"That I don't know," Jack replied. "I suspect that Allison might be behind the exhumation, but how that could impact you beats me. It's possible that she is pulling strings in your department, putting some pressure on you in order to get to me. But I don't know why she would do that unless she suspects I'm holding some of her money.

"Reg did receive a substantial payment—in gold—from Allison. But he was killed before he could pay me. She must not know that. My advice to you, actually it applies to both of us, don't talk to anyone about it."

"Sounds like the right plan. I don't have any info about that anyway."

"Roger's people cleaned up after we left the scene of the shooting. He removed Reg's body and staged a natural death elsewhere. All you need to say is that I rescued you from the kidnappers. Just leave it at that. They may exhume Reg's body, and that should not change anything as far as we're concerned."

"How about Reg's wife?" Kate asked. "What will her reaction be? What's she got to lose or to gain?"

"That gold simply disappeared, as far as I know. I have no idea what Reg did with it before he died. My gut tells me that Pam knows more than she's letting on. I can't imagine Reg not making provisions for her. But, I know nothing for sure."

"Maybe the less we know, the better," Kate added.

"Well, there's absolutely nothing we can do from here."

"Not exactly the case," Kate said.

"What do you mean?"

"They're sending an officer all the way up here to take a deposition."

"You've got to be kidding. What could they possibly think you know that warrants spending all that money just to question you way up here?"

"We're going to find out. And sooner rather than later."

"When?"

"As soon as I give them a date at the county courthouse."

Jack and Kate had parked in the lot of the local Paradise grocery store and there waited for the sheriff and the fire equipment to go past.

The explosion had occurred at the very edge of Chippewa County, so Jack knew the sheriff and the rest of the responders from Chippewa County would have to arrive from that direction.

From the position he had chosen he could also watch for the Escalade, should it for some reason still be in the area.

"There we go," Jack said, pointing at a patrol car screaming up M-123, followed closely by a fire truck and then another ambulance.

"Looks like they are going to find it without our help," Kate observed as the three vehicles turned west toward the site of the explosion.

"Right. But we'd better pull in behind and meet them there. I'm sure they'll have plenty of questions for us, not the least of which will be why we left the scene."

Just after Jack pulled in behind the last of the emergency vehicles, a black Jeep, heading back from State Harbor, slowly slid into traffic and brought up the end of the parade—directly behind Jack.

* * *

"I remember you," the sheriff said to Jack and Kate, as they walked up to the still-smoldering remains of the Gordon vehicle.

Chapter 32

Jack re-encounters "Sheriff" Green

Ａnd I remember you as well," Jack replied with a smile. "Met you at that coffee shop last year. *Deputy* Bill Green, then. Now it's *Sheriff* Green. Congratulations."

"Thanks," Sheriff Green said, carefully considering his next words. "I'd heard that the two of you were in the area. I will have to say that it's been quiet around here—with you gone. This is the first major incident since you guys shot the old sheriff."

Jack chuckled. "That makes us sound pretty menacing when you put it like that."

"Yes it does, and you are. Even though the former sheriff turned out to be a crook *and* a murderer, still there are a lot of my brothers in law enforcement who are not pleased to have you back in town. And now this. What can you tell me about it? And what's your connection?"

"I'm sure you know we called it in," Jack said.

"I do know that. And when we got here you were gone. What exactly was so important that you couldn't wait for us?"

"Sheriff Green," Jack said. "I strongly suspected that the vehicle that was directly behind us remotely triggered the explosion. We were following Mrs. Gordon and her son to have lunch at the brewery."

"That's the names of the victims?" Sheriff Green asked.

"Yes, that's the widow, rather the wife of Tytus Gordon—the diver who went missing yesterday while exploring a new shipwreck."

"And what is your relationship with Mrs. Gordon?"

"There is no relationship. In fact, I hadn't yet had the opportunity to meet her. But her son, Robby, he's a friend of Red, my nephew."

"Did I just hear you refer to Mrs. Gordon as a 'widow'?"

"Slip of the tongue. I take it her husband is still missing?"

"He's dead. And I think you know that. That information has not been released to the public. I would like to know how you knew about it."

It did not take Jack long to conclude that it would not be wise to mislead the sheriff. Jack knew he had more enemies than friends up here, and being less than candid with the sheriff would certainly make winning him over more difficult.

"I did know. I have a friend who is a federal agent, Secret Service, and he told me that the *Snoopy* had been scuttled west of here."

"What's the Secret Service have to do with the sinking of a boat up here in the UP?"

"Nothing whatsoever," Jack replied. "My friend simply has a lot of years in the Service and a lot of contacts. When I want some info on a case, I call him."

"And just how is this *your* case?"

"It's not," Jack said. "It's just that Red and Robby were at camp together this past week. Robby had to go home early when his dad went missing. Mrs. Gordon came up to the camp yesterday and pulled him out. Red was worried, so I promised to do what I could to get to the bottom of it. I called my friend, and he filled me in on what was available to him at that time. He told me that the boat was found, mostly sunk, at Little Lake Harbor, about twenty miles west. I'm sure you've heard that."

"What else did he tell you?"

"I understand that there were a number of bodies on the boat," Jack replied, "and another one in a burned out vehicle a couple miles from the boat. Does that sound about right?"

"Who am I to argue with a Secret Service Agent? I'm just the sheriff of this county, and Little Lake is out of my jurisdiction. And I have to tell you, Handler, I'm not happy to have you poking around in my business. And those bodies in the sunken boat—how were they murdered? Did your friend tell you that?"

"No, as a matter of fact, he didn't tell me how they died. Do you know?"

"I'm not going to discuss this with you further," Sheriff Green said. "But what can you tell me about this car bomb, or whatever it was?"

Chapter 33

Sheriff Green questions Jack about Escalade

Kate, Red, and I were following Mrs. Gordon and her son to the restaurant at the Upper Falls. Red was actually texting the son at the time of the explosion.

"I would guess that the explosive device was under the front seat or maybe between them. The only thing that saved the boy's life was that he was texting Red. Robby had climbed into the back of the vehicle and was messing with Red texting. Had he been seated next to his mother, he would have suffered the same fate.

"When the explosion occurred I immediately pulled over and got out."

"Were you injured in any way?"

"No, not at all. In fact, I don't think there's a mark on my SUV, aside from some harmless debris. I know I didn't hear anything strike it. As soon as I got out I started seeing body parts. I didn't hold out much hope that the woman could have survived the blast. I was hoping that the boy came out okay. I figured he could have since he was so far from the device. And that's how it turned out."

"I suppose you know that the mother didn't make it?"

"I assumed that was the case. It was immediately obvious that there was nothing I could do to help her. That's why I concentrated on finding the boy. He looked to me like his injuries were superficial, except for that burn on his back. I'd guess that was a third degree. He'll be okay, don't you think?"

"Burns were a little more than superficial. If they keep him from going into shock, and if we can get him to a place where they can help him, then I think he'll be okay. But right now, anything can still happen."

"It was then, when I first pulled over, that I noticed that a black Escalade had stopped behind me and was backing up rapidly. I had spotted it a bit earlier. Then it was practically on my rear bumper."

"Did you get the plate?" the sheriff asked.

"Couldn't," Jack replied. "He must have run in reverse over a hundred yards before he turned around. And when he did, he really jammed it. By the time I was able to pursue, he had a fifteen-minute jump on me. When we reached Paradise, I had no way to tell which way he turned—south toward the Soo or north toward Whitefish Point. I still don't know.

"If he headed north, toward the point, he really would have no way out. Not without a boat. So we looked around a little south of town but did not see anything. That's when we decided we'd better wait for you."

"Was there anything about the Escalade that stood out?" the sheriff asked.

"The side glass was lightly tinted, and so was the rear. It was clean, like it hadn't been driven on any dirt roads. If I were to hazard a guess, I'd say it was a rental, or maybe stolen … *probably* stolen, and probably from around here. A rental would be too easy to trace. And if I were to guess again, I'd say that it's already been ditched."

"What did the occupants look like? Did you get a good look at them?"

"No. Only through my rearview mirror, before the explosion. I do recall there were at least two of them, perhaps more. The driver appeared to be large, at least he took up a lot of windshield. The passenger in the front seat was smaller. Both wore sunglasses."

"Were they white guys, or black? Were they wearing anything on their heads—hats, caps?"

"White. My guess is that the driver might have been in his forties—maybe fifties. That's just a guess, of course. They wore sunglasses, but not hats."

As Sheriff Green and Jack talked a black Jeep pulled up behind Jack's SUV, and three well-dressed middle-aged men got out. Two were wearing Tiger caps, and the third was wearing a yellow CAT cap.

Chapter 34

The men in the black Jeep

Gentlemen," the driver of the Jeep said, walking up to where Jack and the sheriff were standing. "We'd heard there was a car on fire down here. We were supposed to meet a friend of ours at the Upper Tahquamenon restaurant. And that looks as though it might be her vehicle. Do you have a name?"

"Sir," Sheriff Green said, walking toward the three men with his hands raised, signaling them to turn around. "Please get back in your vehicle. The road is wide enough, please turn around and head back the way you came. You should consider M-123 shut down. If you need to get to Newberry, you can go back to Paradise and turn right at the signal. Stay on it. It will take you to M-28. There you can turn right, and that'll—"

"I know how to get to Newberry using that route," the Jeep driver said. "But that's not my question. I'm wondering if this is my friend, Mrs. Portage. Can you tell me that much?"

The driver had not turned back. When the sheriff started walking toward him, he then stopped his forward progress, but he never turned around.

"I need you to turn around now," Sheriff Green ordered, "and leave the scene. You can't stay here. And there have been no identifications made. Please leave now."

By that time, the sheriff had reached the three men. The first two had turned around and were heading back to their vehicle. But the driver still persisted.

"I think that's my friend's car," driver said, still not obeying the sheriff's command to leave. "Is it okay if I just get a little closer and check out the plate? That really looks like my friend's car. Was there a teenage boy with her? That would be her son. Was there a child in the car?"

That got Jack's attention. Jack surmised that this fellow was on a fishing trip—trying to force the sheriff's hand into telling him the condition of the passengers.

It just didn't make sense to Jack—altogether too much coincidence. Jack turned toward the driver and took a long look at him.

"The man's lying," Jack said to Kate. "He wasn't meeting anyone. He's just trying to get a confirmation of the kill."

Jack's fixed attention was not wasted. The driver observed Jack's intense stare and suddenly decided that he should vacate the scene.

"Sheriff," Jack said, "I think—"

Chapter 35

Sheriff silences Jack

Y ou shut up too," he shouted over his shoulder in Jack's direction. "Handler, you get back in your car as well."

"Sheriff," Jack continued, "we need to find out—"

"I told you to get back in your vehicle," Sheriff Green barked, this time looking and pointing at Jack. "I'm just about to start throwing people in cuffs around here, so you'd better listen to what I'm saying. The paramedic told me how you assaulted him. I've had just about enough from you. Now get the hell back into your car."

Jack did not comply. Rather he grabbed his cell phone and quickly accessed its camera. Ignoring the Jeep, he turned toward Kate and asked her if she had been listening to what the driver of the Jeep had said regarding his plans to meet a woman and her son at the brewery.

"I heard what he said," Kate replied. "What do you suppose that was all about? I agree he was not on the level. But why he would he lie about that?"

"Tell me when they start to turn around," Jack said, wanting to keep his back turned toward the Jeep until the very last moment.

Kate pretended she was looking at Jack, but she was intently viewing the Jeep over his shoulder.

"Now! They just backed up to turn around," Kate said.

Jack immediately spun around and pointed his cell at the Jeep as it pulled back on the road to Paradise.

"If you'd have warned me, I would have cleaned their plate off so you could have gotten a better picture," Kate joked.

"It was a little muddy, but I'm sure we'll get something—even two or three digits would be better than nothing," Jack replied.

"Handler," the sheriff said, walking back to where Jack was parked. "What were you trying to say?"

"Not much, Sheriff. But you could tell me if you know anything about those fellows you just chased away."

"I don't know them. Do you?"

"Never saw them before," Jack said. "Would you say that they were from around here?"

"I'd guess not," the sheriff replied. "Too pushy, and they were dressed wrong."

"How's that?" Jack asked. "How were they dressed wrong?"

Chapter 36

No place for leather sandals

No one from around here wears those leather sandals. Two of those fellows were wearing them. My guess—they were from Chicago or Detroit. Why is that important to you? Why are you asking about them?"

"The driver said that he was meeting a mother and her son at the brewery to eat. Kate and I were meeting Mrs. Gordon and her son at the brewery for lunch. I'm thinking it's unlikely that his story was true. I think he was just trying to get you to tell him that the name of the deceased was Gordon, not Portage. I think he was lying. In fact, I would not be surprised if he was just trying to get a confirmation of his kill. I think he was a pro."

"You said that the only car you saw around here was a black

Escalade, and that was a Jeep. He was probably just trying to get information to gossip about at the bar tonight. People do that."

Jack was not pleased with the sheriff's unwillingness to listen.

"You're probably right," Jack agreed in frustration. "Perhaps it was nothing."

"Is there anything else you can tell me about that Escalade or its occupants?" Sheriff Green asked.

At this point, Jack realized that his experience and understanding of the situation gave him the upper hand. With his green eyes piercing the sheriff's reflective sunglasses, Jack went into autopilot.

For the moment, Jack traveled back in time. He was seated on the witness stand. And instead of speaking to a county sheriff, he was addressing a Chicago jury, methodically reporting each detail.

"I recall that there were two good-sized men. No hats. Well groomed. When the Escalade turned around I noticed the side windows were tinted. But they backed so far down the road I couldn't catch the plate, except that it was Michigan. Interestingly, the place they chose to turn around was exactly the same one that the Jeep just used."

Chapter 37

From Escalade to Jeep?

The sheriff knew then that he had messed up.

"You think that the fellows who got out of the Jeep were the same ones you earlier saw in the Caddy? That's what you're suggesting, isn't it?"

"That's a definite possibility—the original two, plus one. The plus one was perhaps the driver who picked them up after they ditched the Escalade. Just speculation."

The sheriff walked over to his vehicle and radioed in for any cars in the area to be watching for a black 2010 Jeep Wrangler with three men—possibly headed south on M-123.

The sun was blazing down on the blacktop, producing beads of perspiration on Jack's forehead.

"You get a plate on that, Handler?" he yelled over at Jack.

"I took a picture, but it was pretty far away," Jack replied. "I'll email it to you. Maybe your guys can enhance it."

"Just bring your phone over here. Is it a Droid? Maybe we can do a direct file transfer using my Wi-Fi."

Jack complied with Sheriff Green's request and transferred the image to the sheriff's cell.

"That's not a bad image," the sheriff said. "I'll bet we get something useful off that. That's what you were trying to tell me, wasn't it? When I told you to back off?"

"I was just beginning to wonder about those guys. But I didn't know anything for certain. Still don't. It's probably best anyway that they think they're in the clear, don't you think?"

"It would have been best if I'd listened to you. We had them. I should have questioned them. Hey, Jack, I'm just learning the ropes. I went directly from a patrol car to the sheriff's office. I got myself elected, but I'm no detective. Look, any help you can be on this case, and that includes your daughter as well, anything you find out. I would really appreciate your help."

"You got it, Sheriff."

"I know I gave you some attitude earlier," the sheriff said. "But, you and that daughter of yours set this whole county on its side. You killed two of the longest-tenured law enforcement officers in the UP."

"Yes we did, and those shootings were righteous."

"I know that, but Restin and the sheriff had friends. A lot of friends. And when you shoot a law enforcement officer, doesn't matter the situation, when you kill one of us, you make enemies. You and your daughter have real enemies up here. And I'm the first to admit that I have mixed feelings about you two as well."

"That's honest," Jack said. "I appreciate your candor. And, if I were in your shoes, I'd undoubtedly feel the same way. But you have to realize that both Deputy Restin and the sheriff were criminals— *hard-core* criminals ... professional art thieves ... and murderers.

"Either one of them would have put a bullet in you if they thought it would help them. And in both cases, they would have killed us had we not defended ourselves."

"I know. I know. But—"

Before Sheriff Green could complete his thought, he got a call on his radio: "Sheriff Green, we've got a hit on the plate you sent us."

Chapter 38

Now that's interesting!

That was fast," the sheriff said, responding to the call. "Whatcha got for me? Wait. Hang on for a second. We need to keep this private."

Sheriff Green then slipped in a wireless earbud.

"Okay, fire away."

For nearly a full minute, the sheriff was totally silent on his end. Finally, he opened his door and sat down in his patrol car. His red and blue strobes defined the pavement beneath him, as well as tree lines a hundred feet away, as a crime scene.

Passersby—keep your distance.

"Explain that to me again. If you couldn't make out the full plate, how can you be so certain you've got this right?"

"Six of seven characters match? And it's on his Jeep? And it's a black Jeep? Well, I'd say that was pretty positive. Good work. Put that plate and vehicle description out. To the state boys too. I'd like to find that car as quickly as possible."

Sheriff Green remained seated for several more seconds, and then he removed the earbud and walked over to where Jack was standing.

"Ready for this?" he asked Jack. " I'll admit that *I* wasn't."

"You got an ID on that plate?"

"Sure did," the sheriff said. "Glad you captured that image. Well, this is what we found out. My guys were able to positively identify six of the seven characters, and they match a plate from a 2010 black Jeep Wrangler registered to Dr. Wilbur Henry. He's a professor at the Lake Superior Archaeological Center. From what I can tell, right now, he was supposed to have been on the boat with Gordon yesterday. He was Gordon's principal skeptic. But he didn't go. Instead, he sent his assistant and a deep-sea photographer."

Dr. Henry was greatly respected in the academic community. He had done his undergraduate work at Brandeis and earned both his master's degree and PhD from the University of Pennsylvania. His field of interest in college was anthropology, but he had obtained his doctorate in archaeology.

He had written his doctoral dissertation on pre-classical Greek archaeology. So when he was offered a position by the Archaeological Center to chair its department of archaeology, none of his colleagues quite understood why he would consider it.

What they didn't know was that Dr. Henry tried but could not find a suitable position more directly related to his field of expertise. The 1970s were tough. Universities, even the biggest and the best of them, did not have the funds to add to their staffs.

But it worked out well for Dr. Henry. Even though he found it very difficult to access original source material in his field, he still managed to publish in respectable journals. Often he contacted friends who were employed by major research universities and used them to help him gain access to pertinent documents and artifacts. It was a tough way to do research, but he managed.

After more than thirty years as the chair of his department, he was preparing to retire. If ever there were a perfect example of a big fish in a little pond, Dr. Henry was it.

"Those three fellows who got out of the Jeep," Jack said. "I could be wrong, but none of them looked like a college professor to me. They look like tenured eggheads to you?"

"Hardly," the sheriff agreed.

"Any word on the professor?"

Chapter 39

Tracking down the Jeep

He's in Houghton, right now," the sheriff said. "And he taught classes all day yesterday. He has a summer cottage just west of Whitefish Point. More specifically, it's off West Northshore Road, according to what I'm bringing up here. It's a road called Cemetery Road. It runs between West Northshore and Wild Cat Road. I don't think I've ever run a call to Cemetery Road. Must be nice, though. That's where Dr. Henry lives."

"I'm sure you ran the plates to see if the Jeep was reported stolen?"

"It's not on any list," the sheriff said. "But it's possible that the professor kept the Jeep at his cottage, and so he might not even know if it was stolen."

"You know that for a fact? That he kept the Jeep at his cottage?"

"Don't know it for a fact," the sheriff replied. "But a Jeep Wrangler seems more like an amusement vehicle for the professor than his regular means of transportation around campus. Wouldn't you agree?"

"I'd like to see it checked out," Jack replied.

"We're on it right now. Where's that daughter of yours?"

"I'm sure she's with Robby. And I think I saw her taking Red over there as well. Would you mind if she and Red rode in the ambulance with the boy?"

"I wouldn't mind, but the paramedics might. I heard that you roughed one of them up pretty good. Is that true?"

"Absolutely not. I just wanted to get my point across, and he was less than attentive."

"Oh, well, then I suppose I fully understand. He wanted to do his job, and you wanted to get in his face. That makes perfect sense to me."

"Would you please clear it with them to allow Kate and Red to ride with the boy. He's just lost both parents. He needs to have some friendly faces around him right now."

"I'll take care of it."

"Thanks. Say, Sheriff, do you have a problem with my checking up on those fellows a little bit on my own? Those guys in the Jeep?"

Chapter 40

Kate flirts

I want my mom," Robby mouthed, still not aware that his mother had died in the explosion. He could not speak clearly because of a breathing tube, but both Red and Kate knew what he was trying to say.

The paramedics were painstakingly making sure all the boy's vital signs were stabilized before they attempted to transport him—standard protocol dictated it.

Robby strongly protested when the paramedics placed him in a cervical collar, so the decision was made to administer a mild sedative. Amazingly, he showed no evidence of serious head trauma even though he had been launched like a missile through the roof of an exploding vehicle.

In addition to the neck brace and breathing tube, they hooked him up to an intravenous line to maintain hydration. They then carefully cleaned all his wounds, particularly the more severely burned area on his back.

"What's the prognosis?" Kate asked the paramedic who was riding in the back with them. "We're headed to the Soo, right?"

"That's right. We'll get him in and let the doctor take a look at his burns. He will confer with the rest of the staff, and then a determination will be made as to where and how the boy will be treated."

"What do you mean by *where*?"

"Most of his burns are second degree. But some are more serious. We have to be very concerned about infections. If the doctors think it best, he will be transported to a burn center. Don't know whether or not that'll be the decision. But it could be."

"Where is the closest burn center?"

Chapter 41

The DMC?

G enerally, with children, we like the Pediatric Burn Center at the DMC—that's the Detroit Medical Center."

"You mean you might drive him all the way to Detroit?"

"We probably wouldn't, but someone might. They might even fly him there. But if the doctors think he can be properly treated here, then that's what will happen. Those types of decisions are way above my pay grade. We just make sure the patient is stabilized, with a breathing tube, and we make sure he's hydrated. And, of course, we clean him up a bit. But that's about it. Can't do much more."

Kate then buckled herself into the seat and helped Red do the same.

"What's your gut with Robby? Do you think that they will recommend sending him down to Detroit?"

"Like I said, those decisions are not ours to make. Not even ours to speculate on. But I would say that I think his overall prognosis is very good. At least that's what my experience tells me. If we can keep the infections out. That's the biggest danger, at this point. But I think you can be very optimistic."

"I appreciate your openness," Kate said. "I really do. And I greatly appreciate the care you have taken with our young friend."

"Just doin' my job. But I do appreciate your kind words. Don't always hear the positive comments."

Kate looked the paramedic in the eyes and flashed him her best smile. It won him over.

Kate was more than just a beautiful woman. While all first impressions are based heavily upon appearances, the more a person got to know about Kate, the higher the opinion of her.

She did not have to talk a lot. Actually, she did far more listening than talking. So when she did open her mouth, she got attention.

One of the reasons she moved up so quickly in the New York detective ranks was her ability to converse intelligently in several languages. She could read a suspect his rights in Spanish, Arabic, and Greek, as well as in several Southeast Asian dialects.

Add to all of those other attributes, her large green eyes, thick auburn hair, and a gorgeously fit martial-arts trimmed body, and you can begin to understand just how imposing a figure Kate was.

So when she smiled at the paramedic, he melted.

And that's exactly the reaction she wanted. She knew just how rough her father had treated them, and she wanted to make up for some of it.

Besides, she was truly grateful for the service the paramedics had provided Robby, and wanted it to continue.

"Aren't you two a perfect pair," Kate said, turning her attention back to Red and Robby.

Placing the tip of her right index finger on the end of Red's nose, she said, "You, my favorite cousin, can't talk." And then placing that same finger on Robby's nose, said "and you can't talk *or* hear."

"I can hear," Robby mouthed. "I can hear now."

"Wonderful!" Kate exclaimed. "Already you're getting better. What great news."

Kate was pleased that Robby was beginning to hear again. But with his getting that sense back, she was left with a greater challenge in dealing with his questions about his mother.

"Why are we stopping?" Kate asked, as everything in the ambulance that was not secured abruptly shifted forward.

"Not sure," the paramedic said. "I'll check."

"What the hell!" he said, looking through the opening and viewing a disturbance in front of the ambulance.

Chapter 42

A not so funny thing happened

Open up!" boomed a voice at the rear of the ambulance. The shouting was followed by a muscular pounding on the door.

"Kate Handler! We know you're back there. Don't try anything foolish. If you do, you'll get both of those boys killed. Just unlock this door and open it up. I promise that no one will get hurt if you do. We just need to talk to you."

"What shall we do?" the paramedic asked. "You're a cop, right? What should we do?"

"We open it up. We don't have a choice. They will hurt your buddy up front, and then these kids. We don't have a choice."

Kate was in Michigan. She had no authority outside of New York

City. And she was not armed. Because state firearm laws regarding law enforcement personnel from other states are often murky, Kate decided that she would not test them. Therefore, she did not even bring a handgun on the trip.

Besides, she was traveling with her dad, and she knew her father would be armed. Even though he was retired from Chicago law enforcement, because Michigan was a bordering state, he maintained a permit to carry concealed in that state as well.

However, even if she were armed, her position was untenable. The driver was already a hostage, and the two young boys were much too vulnerable.

"What in the world could they want with me?" she said. "Go ahead, open the door."

Kate quickly learned that she was not the target.

Chapter 43

Jack in slow pursuit

What are the chances?" Jack kept asking himself.

He knew that the odds were great that his effort to catch up with the mysterious Jeep would fail. But that did not deter him—often persistence produces results.

He also knew that there was little to learn or gain by sticking around with the sheriff. Familiarity breeds contempt, he reasoned. And his relationship with this sheriff could easily devolve into one rank with contention.

Jack was convinced that the sheriff was not intentionally bucking him. Yet, every time they appeared to be agreeing about something, the sheriff found a way to push Jack back.

Jack was convinced that the sheriff wanted to take advantage of his expertise but was afraid to.

Up until the recent election that catapulted Bill Green into the sheriff's office, Deputy Green had always been a pretty pedestrian patrolman. Granted, he was highly effective in that position. But his day-to-day responsibilities were still those of a patrolman.

After the big blowup precipitated by the deaths of the corrupt sheriff and his chief deputy, Bill emerged from the hullabaloo without a blemish. Not only did he have the support of Sault Ste. Marie and Chippewa County officials, but he was well liked and respected among his peers. So, even though he lacked leadership experience, when he ran for sheriff he did so unopposed within the department.

Now Sheriff Bill had to walk a fine line. Anger and mistrust permeated not only his office (regarding the killing of two county law enforcement officers), but those same emotions poisoned many of the relationships the sheriff tried to develop throughout the entire UP.

So, for Sheriff Bill to cozy up to Jack and Kate would mean new pressures for him.

That's why Jack was eager to keep out of his way. If and when he came up with some new information he would give the county a call. But the rest of the time he would work with Kate and do his best to keep his distance from local officials—particularly the sheriff. At least that was his plan.

Okay, now that could be interesting, Jack said to himself, his adrenalin building.

That sure as hell looks like my Jeep! Could it be?

Chapter 44

Yeah, I'm a cop!

The Jeep Jack had spotted was parked next to a small but popular gas station/convenience store on the south end of Paradise.

"They sure aren't in much of a hurry," Jack muttered, pulling in and stopping near the road, about 150 feet from the Jeep.

He waited there until the three men emerged from the store. It was the same men who had asked so many questions at the scene of the explosion.

"Candy bars and Cokes," Jack quipped to himself. "Obviously not cops—no doughnuts."

Jack took his foot off the brake and gunned his engine, throwing gravel with his spinning tires.

All three men stopped in their tracks, thinking that he was going to ram the rear of their Jeep.

Jack then slammed on his brakes and skidded right up to within inches of the parked vehicle. And he got out.

"What the hell was that all about?" The driver asked. "And who the hell are you?"

"My name is Jack. And I've got some questions for you."

The driver was angry and started walking into Jack's face.

"Get your car outta my way, or I'll move it for you."

"Do whatever you think you have to, sport," Jack said, placing his hands on his hips, spreading his jacket just enough to expose a twenty-year-old badge and a holstered .38 S&W Special stainless steel revolver.

"You a cop?" the driver said, stopping in his tracks.

Jack then took two steps in the driver's direction, placed his right hand on the side of the Jeep, and said, "Yup. Now, what was it you were saying? You're gonna move my car for me? Well, the keys are in it, and the engine's running. Why don't you go for it?"

"Ray," one of the passengers called over. "Just see what he wants. We don't need any trouble."

The passenger who spoke with authority had been sitting in the backseat. He had waited there while the other three men went into the store.

Ray was not eager to back down, but he also did not want a confrontation with a cop. So he chose to square off with Jack, but at a safe distance.

"You had a lot of questions about that accident a little while ago. What was that all about?"

"Accident? That didn't look much like an accident to me."

"Just how do you know the Gordons. Were they friends of yours?"

"Ray, talk to the man," the passenger commanded as he got out of the Jeep and began walking back to where Ray and Jack were standing. "We've got nothing to hide."

Jack's gut told him these men did not pose a threat. Yet, decades of dealing with Chicago criminals had taught him to be wary of numbers.

"Hold it right there!" Jack barked, holding up his right hand toward the passenger while he was still on the far side of the Jeep. "I'll get to you in a minute. I want you to get back into the car right now and wait there."

Jack then reached down and unsnapped his revolver.

Jack was a little surprised, but pleased, that the passenger immediately obeyed him. That suggested the men had not been drinking. And it also indicated a willingness of the leader to cooperate.

Chapter 45

Jack turns his attention to passenger

Okay, Ray, just who's in charge here?" Jack asked. "You, or your old man?"

Jack had observed that the other man looked to be about a dozen years older than the driver. And by the way, the passenger ordered the driver around, it was clear to Jack that he was talking to the wrong man.

"Never mind, Ray. You get back in the car and stay there until I tell you otherwise. Do it! Now. Get back behind the wheel. But do not start your engine."

Ray did as he was told, but he left his door open to expedite reengagement, were he to deem it necessary.

Jack then walked behind the Jeep and over to the passenger side.

The older man had sat down on the seat but had left his door open and had both feet on the ground.

"Now, what's your name?" Jack asked. "And how are you connected to the Gordons?"

"My name is Wilbur Henry, Dr. Wilbur Henry."

"Really?" Jack said. "Weren't you supposed to be on that boat? The one that didn't make it back in last night?"

"That's right. I was scheduled to go out with Mr. Gordon and observe his so-called discovery."

"You didn't accept his conclusions about it. Isn't that right? You did not believe the wreck to be a Minoan vessel."

"It *couldn't* have been," the professor snarled.

It was clear to Jack that he had touched a nerve.

"Why did you cancel out on the trip?" Jack asked.

"Look. I can't go running all over the country every time some crackpot claims to have found something. Besides, I really did not like this Gordon guy. He had no credentials. He was not a *real* scholar. No one in our—"

"You *didn't* like him?" Jack interrupted. "Past tense? Has something happened that now makes you like him? What did you mean by that?"

"We both know that the man is dead," the professor said.

"What makes you say that?" Jack asked.

"I heard gunshots. I was on the radio with my associate. He was on the boat at the site of the alleged wreck. They were just lowering the exploration sub. We were talking. And then, all of a sudden, there was automatic gunfire."

"Automatic? Are you sure it was automatic?"

"It was rapid. You know: pop pop pop pop. Like one continuous sound. My associate said something like, 'Oh my god. He just shot Gordon!' And then the radio went dead. I don't know anything else about it."

"Did you inform the sheriff about what you heard?"

"No. I wanted to see what I could learn first."

"Who's the muscle? Who's this Ray guy?"

"Ray works for me."

"In what capacity?"

"He's head of a security company out of Detroit, and he does some work for me from time to time."

"You mean like a bodyguard?"

"No. It's nothing like that. Ray's a friend. Sometimes, when I get into a sketchy situation, Ray comes along to make sure everything turns out okay."

"Did you consider Mr. Gordon to be a threat?"

"Not so much. But there was just something about this whole situation that made me feel uncomfortable."

"What do you mean by that? What was it about Mr. Gordon that made you *uncomfortable*?"

"*He* didn't. But there were some other fellows, shady fellows. They were trouble."

"Were they friends of Mr. Gordon?"

"Not friends. He was even more worried about them than I was."

These are not my bombers, Jack thought as he prepared to move on.

Just then Jack's cell phone signaled a text. He looked down and, seeing that it was Kate texting him, asked to see the professor's drivers license.

Dr. Henry complied with Jack's request and handed him his

license.

Jack took it and walked back to his vehicle. His intention was to hang on to the professor's drivers license in case he had to reach him later.

Chapter 46

Sorry—gotta go

U nk Jack help."

Jack was not proficient at texting. In fact, it was only because of Red that Jack even attempted to learn how to do it.

"Where R U?"

"25 minuts"

"R U ok"

"IM ok. Help"

"On my way," Jack replied.

Jack did not take the time to excuse himself. He shoved his vehicle into drive and took off.

"Hey," Ray yelled as Jack shot off the gravel and sped south down

Highway M-123. "Where you goin'?"

Jack slid the professor's drivers license into his empty ashtray and began to calculate how far the ambulance might have traveled in twenty-five minutes.

"Twenty-five minutes at fifty-five miles an hour," Jack said aloud. "That would put them somewhere past the Scenic Byway, but before Highway 28. Probably *closer* to 28."

The Scenic Byway is officially known as Lake Superior Shoreline Road. It follows the southern shoreline of Whitefish Bay, winding past the picturesque Iroquois Point Lighthouse, Bay Mills Resort and Casino, and a very popular Native American coffee shop—The Dancing Crane. Eventually, it runs into Highway 221, which swings back to Highway M-28.

Jack thought about it and concluded that if someone pulled the ambulance over, they would make sure they could quickly get it off the main road and out of sight.

Jack texted: "On main road?"

"Dirt," was Red's immediate response.

"Right or left," Jack fired back.

"???"

"Can U see road?"

"No. Hnds tied."

"I'll find U."

"I no."

Then Jack asked Red if he could identify the vehicle.

Red texted: "Black Jeep."

When Jack read it he bellowed out loud, "Another damn black Jeep. I guess we are in the Upper Peninsula!"

Jack passed the Scenic Route road that led off toward Brimley before he slowed down.

Should be farther down than this, but maybe not that much, Jack said to himself. *Sure be nice to know which side of the road I should look.*

Five more minutes passed. And then Jack received another text: "Right."

At first Red had not understood what Jack meant. After Red had some time to think about it, he realized what his uncle was asking.

"Okay!" Jack shouted. "That helps."

Chapter 47

The Excitement never ends

J ack intently scrutinized every track that appeared to head west off of M-123 but found none fresh enough to satisfy him. He knew that a vehicle as large as an ambulance would create substantial depressions on a dirt road, particularly with the dual rear wheels.

A thought suddenly came to him, and Jack slammed on the brakes.

About a mile back, and just before Red had identified the suspect vehicle, Jack had encountered a dark SUV headed back into Paradise. The longer he thought about it, the more likely it seemed to him that the vehicle he had seen was the dark Jeep described by Red.

He just sat there motionless in the middle of the southbound lane. He was faced with a dilemma—should he pursue the Jeep, or rescue Kate and Red?

"Sure you guys OK? U & Kate?" Jack texted.

"IM fine cnt c Kate."

"B ther soon. Thnk I saw Jeep."

Jack checked his mirror and saw a vehicle approaching from behind.

"Time to move," he said. Whipping his vehicle around, he headed back toward Paradise.

Soon after he passed the point at which he figured he had seen the Jeep, he noticed vehicle tracks heading off M-123 to the west.

"Those tracks were not there before," Jack muttered. "I would have seen them."

Jack slammed on his brakes again and checked his mirror, shoved his vehicle in reverse, and backed up to where he had spotted them.

Instead of turning into the drive, he pulled off onto the shoulder on the opposite side of the road and got out.

It was as he suspected. Clearly the tracks he spotted were made by an off-road vehicle—quite possibly a Jeep—traveling at a high rate of speed.

And they were made recently.

But the curious thing about it was the tracks on top of them—even fresher tracks.

Chapter 48

It has Jack going in circles

The off-road tracks indicated that the vehicle making them had approached from the south and slid wildly off the drive.

However, the tracks made afterward were not those of an SUV, and they did not evidence speed or recklessness.

Instead, those tracks were made by a front wheel drive, probably full-size vehicle. It had come to a complete stop at the road and then pulled out without spinning.

Both sets of tracks had been created after Jack had initially driven past that drive in his effort to rescue Red and Kate.

"Oh my god!" Jack exclaimed. That would have been the car that pulled up behind me when I was turning around. This is starting to make me dizzy."

Jack did another U-turn and headed south down M-123.

"Sheriff. Jack Handler here. This is going to take a long time to explain, so I think I'll fill you in later. But for now, this is what I need you to do."

The sheriff did not want to take orders from Jack, even though he knew Jack's suggestions would be worthwhile.

"I understand totally," Jack said, trying to placate the sheriff's ego. "But get this. The ambulance carrying the injured boy, Red and Kate, and the two paramedics. As far as I can tell it was commandeered along 123 somewhere between the Scenic Byway and 28. I suspect that the boy was then transferred to a different vehicle."

The news overwhelmed the sheriff, and he suddenly became willing to hear Jack out.

"This is what I need you to do," Jack said.

Chapter 49

Jack admits mistake

First of all, let me just put it this way. I screwed up, and I need you to bail me out. I let the car with the hijackers get past me. I had them right there in front of me and let them go. It is a dark colored, possibly dark blue or black, full-sized sedan. I'm thinking Buick, but I can't be sure about that. It's got a ten-minute head start. The occupants have no reason to think they've been made, so they're likely to be driving within speed limits.

"The last I saw them they were about six miles north of Highway M-28, headed south. I would imagine either you or the state have vehicles in the vicinity. I have no idea how many occupants. But it's possible that they've kidnaped the boy—Robby. Why else would they have stopped the ambulance, if not for the boy? And, I'm not sure about Kate. It's possible she might be with the boy."

Jack was happy to disconnect the call.

"Okay, this is where I turned around. I should spot a few sets of fresh tracks headed off to the west, the dual tires from the ambulance should be quite easy to distinguish.

"Wow!" Jack exclaimed, pulling to the side to allow two sheriff's vehicles to shoot past. "That didn't take long!"

Jack took an extra moment to watch the speeding patrol cars disappear to the south. Just before he pulled back onto the road, his eyes followed down a narrow dirt road leading off into the woods.

About twenty-five feet back from the main road he spotted vehicle tracks—including tracks made by an off-road vehicle, as well as those of a dual-rear-wheeled vehicle.

"That's my ambulance!" Jack exclaimed.

"Well don't that just about beat all," Jack chuckled. "Those fellows took the time to cover up their tracks."

Just off the dirt road laid a small tree that had recently been broken off at ground level. The kidnappers had carefully used its leafy limbs to obscure their tracks close to the road.

Jack marveled at the coincidence. Had he not been forced to pull over at that exact moment, he would not have so quickly located the dirt road texted him by Red.

He wasted no time. He knew the odds were great that no one with bad intentions remained with the ambulance. And, Red had already texted him that no one at that site had been injured. He supposed that included the two paramedics. Even anticipating nothing but good news awaiting him at this juncture, Jack remained wary of what might lie ahead.

Chapter 50

Proceeding with caution

J ack pulled onto the dirt road and peered ahead as far as he could see. The road curved sharply to the right about one hundred yards in. Beyond that point, he was blind.

As he approached the abrupt turn in the road, he stopped. Pulling his revolver out of the holster, he verified that it was fully loaded with .38 Special rounds. The .38 S&W Special revolver that he carried could accommodate .357 caliber cartridges, but he preferred the lower velocity .38s for this sort of circumstance. The more powerful rounds are capable of passing through an entire vehicle and causing catastrophic damage on the other side. *This,* he reasoned, *was not the appropriate application for that type of firepower.*

Once satisfied he had the proper setup of his pistol, he reached into the center console and pulled out two speedloaders. Verifying that they each contained six .38 Special rounds, he slid them into his left jacket pocket.

Jack did not return his pistol to its holster. Instead, he left it between his legs so he could get to it in a hurry if need be. He then proceeded up the dirt road.

Jack was a little surprised that he had not yet spotted the ambulance. After driving nearly a quarter of a mile back into the woods, he could finally see it ahead.

He stopped his vehicle between two large oak trees about fifty yards back, making sure it completely blocked the road. He got out and walked slowly toward the ambulance.

"The only reason they would have driven so far off the road," Jack reasoned, was so that they would have a lot of privacy."

Jack knew that could be bad news.

By the time he was about thirty yards away, he spotted the body of a man lying directly behind the ambulance. He lifted his pistol to firing position, gripping it with both hands, and continued his cautious approach.

Even though the doors on the rear of the ambulance were wide open, it was parked at such an acute angle that he could not see inside.

When he reached a point about twenty feet from the first body, he stopped and knelt down to get a bit of a look underneath the vehicle.

Just then he noticed movement—the man on the ground turned his head toward him.

Chapter 51

Jack gets a surprise

Initially, the man's face was pointing away from Jack's approach. Now it was turned in his direction. Jack recognized him.

"At least one of them is alive," Jack muttered to himself.

He could see the man trying to get a look at him. But just as Red had texted, the culprits had employed duct tape to render them helpless.

Jack knew the man could see him, so he held up his left index finger to signal him to remain still.

Jack stood to his feet and continued slowly toward the ambulance.

When he reached the man on the ground, Jack immediately recognized him. It was the paramedic he had roughed up earlier.

Jack again signaled the man to remain silent. And then he carefully removed the duct tape from over his mouth.

"Is anyone watching you?" Jack asked.

The man shook his head no.

"Is Kate, my daughter, is she okay?"

"I think so," he said. "They had guns, but I did not hear any shots. I hope she's okay. But I don't know."

Jack did not free the man's hands or feet. Not yet. He knew that if a gunman were still there, the paramedic would be better off not moving around. Plus, right now Jack wanted no interference.

"They inside the ambulance?" Jack asked.

"Don't know. They put a cloth over my face—chloroform, I think. I don't know where the others are."

"You just lie here and be quiet. I'll get back to you."

Jack thought that to be good news. Chloroform, properly administered, is safer for the victims than most other modes of rendering them helpless. Too many times attackers try to knock the victim out and the blow turns out fatal.

The paramedic acknowledged Jack's command with a nod.

Still with his weapon at the ready, Jack approached the rear doors of the ambulance. Less than a foot from the opening Jack spotted Red's bare foot. He then looked down, and saw one of the fourteen-year-old boy's shoes, strings still tied, lying on the ground.

"Red. Don't make a sound," Jack commanded.

Red was not about to make a sound—he still had tape over his mouth.

Carefully, Jack bent down and removed the tape from Red's face. He also freed his hands and feet.

Jack observed a cell phone lying beside Red and immediately

surmised how the boy had managed to text him.

"This is Kate's cell phone, right?" Jack asked.

Red nodded.

"Is she around?"

Red shrugged his shoulders.

"Sit still, son, and be quiet. I'm gonna look around a bit."

Chapter 52

Jack searches for Kate

J ack stood to get a better look inside the ambulance. The blood-stained transport stretcher remained secured, but Robby was not in it.

And Kate was not around either.

"Red, do you have any idea where Kate might be?"

Red shook his head no.

"Did they put you to sleep?"

Red nodded.

Kate intentionally dropped her cell phone, and you used your toes to reach it. Right?"

Red nodded.

Red's hands had been secured to one of the permanent metal

structural braces inside the ambulance. While he was unable to use his hands to get his own cell phone out of his pocket, somehow the boy did manage to strip off his shoe and sock and retrieve Kate's cell phone from the ground.

That was no accident, Jack concluded. *Kate knew Red would come through, and so she left her cell phone within reach for him to use once he woke up.*

Jack at this point was fairly certain none of the attackers remained. But he still had to find the second paramedic, Kate, and Robby.

It did not take long to find the second medical technician. Jack spotted him lying on the ground about fifteen feet from the edge of the dirt road. Fate was not so kind to him.

Chapter 53

The search for Kate and Robby continues

A s soon as Jack approached the man, he knew there was a problem. The man's eyes were open, with his pupils dilated and fixed. The second paramedic was dead.

Jack knelt beside him and pressed his fingers against the man's neck. There was no pulse.

Running out of his nose were what appeared to be stomach fluids and small chunks of partially digested food.

Jack correctly surmised that the man for some reason vomited, and with the duct tape over his mouth, he had inhaled the vomit.

"Poor bastard," Jack mumbled.

Realizing that this was now a murder scene, he did not further touch the dead man, nor remove the duct tape from his face.

Jack then went back to the first paramedic and freed him.

"Your associate wasn't so lucky," he said.

"Whaddya mean?"

"He's dead."

"No! Larry can't be dead! Are you sure?"

"Positive. And I'm telling you that you can't go to him, can't touch him, or anything like that at all. There's likely to be finger-prints, or some DNA. The police will have to take care of him. Just know that Larry is no longer here. The body over there isn't your friend. That body is now a piece of evidence—*important* evidence. Do you understand what I am saying?"

The man nodded.

Jack helped the man up, led him over to the rear of the ambu-lance, and sat him down.

"Now, I want you to tell me everything you remember about what happened to Kate and the other boy."

Chapter 54

Too many questions —not enough answers

S heriff. Handler here. I found the ambulance. But not all is so good."

"What does that mean?" Sheriff Green asked.

"One of the paramedics is alive and well, and so is Red, my nephew. That's the good news.

"The bad news is that my daughter and the Gordon boy are missing. And the second technician is dead. Any luck with the Buick? I saw you shoot past me about twenty minutes ago."

"The state police got a roadblock up on M-123 just north of Trout Lake. They had a car in the vicinity, so that worked well. I think they set up within a few minutes of when you first reported it to me. Don't think it leaked in that direction.

"I had a car about nine miles east of the east stretch of M-123 on M-28. Also got that secured within a few minutes.

"Right now I'm on M-123 *at* M-28. Nothing got past me on the way here. I just wish I had good news about 28 west of 123.

"The nearest officer in that direction was just west of Newberry when he got the call. It was a state car. He hightailed it to the east side of Newberry and set up there."

"Why is that *bad* news?" Jack asked.

"Because that's a long stretch, from M-123 to Newberry. Plenty of places to hide out. Now, I don't think it's likely that they got past Newberry to the west, or to the north, and there are really no *main* roads off that stretch of M-123. Plenty of side roads, though. Finding them could be very difficult, if they holed up."

"So, what do you have in mind at this point? I don't want to interfere, but this *is* kidnapping. They took both Kate and the boy. That makes it a federal offense. You've got to call in the FBI sooner or later."

"I've got a call in. It'll take a little time for them to get mobilized. I regarded it as a kidnapping as soon as you told me they grabbed the ambulance."

"Speaking of, I have no idea exactly where we are here. Just north of your position I'd guess. I'm gonna grab Red and head back to where I think they ditched the Jeep. Which would be little further north of where I am right now. I'll mark the dirt road as I pull out. Seems a stretch, but it could be Kate and the Gordon kid got left with the Jeep. I'll leave the surviving paramedic here."

"*You* need to stay there too," the sheriff insisted. "I'll send a deputy as soon as I can. But you wait with the ambulance until he arrives."

"Didn't catch that. We must be losing signal."

Jack then disconnected the call, shut his phone off, and turned his attention to the paramedic.

Chapter 55

Jack questions the paramedic

Tell me as much as you can about the incident. What kind of vehicle were they driving? How'd they stop you? What did they want? What do you recall about Kate. Did they take her with them? And how about the boy?"

The paramedic sat on the back of the ambulance, cradling his head in his hands. He had been crying.

"I don't know. Or I don't really remember. At least not much. I was driving, and this Jeep shot out in front of us. From this road. He made us stop. The next thing I know, a man jumps out of the Jeep, runs over to my door, and pulls me out. Then he forced me to the back of the ambulance. By that time, another man was back there. He was pounding on the back door. He had run around from the other side of the Jeep.

"Someone opened the door. I think it was the woman, Kate. And the man who pulled me out of the front seat then tosses me in the back. The second man gets in back with us. Then the first man drives the ambulance down this dirt road. And that's just about all I really remember. The man in back with us had a gun. The woman was trying to calm the boy down—the victim.

"When we got back here, they make us get out of the ambulance, and they taped us up. And then they knocked me out with chloroform. That's the last thing I remember, period. I don't remember anything about the victim or the woman. Maybe the red head remembers more."

"Can you describe the men? White? Black? What they were wearing? Anything you think might help? What kind of guns did they have? Were their faces covered? Did they speak with an accent?"

"They were wearing nylon stockings over their faces. But I could tell at least two of them were white. I only saw two. The driver stayed in the car, at least as far as I can remember."

"Accents? Did they sound like they were from around here?"

"The one who grabbed me didn't talk—I don't think. The only one I remember saying anything was the second man. He pounded on the back door and ordered them to open it up. I couldn't tell if he had an accent. I'd guess no, but I really couldn't tell. They said so little."

"Are you good if I leave you here? The sheriff has a car on the way."

"I'm fine," the paramedic said.

"You're not fine, Son," Jack said, placing his hand on the man's shoulder. You've been through a lot today. You know, I don't think I got your name."

"William. My name is William Reynolds."

"And what was your friend's name?"

"Larry Thompson, his name is … was … Larry Thompson. He's been my partner for eight years. And he's my roommate."

William then placed his head between his hands and began to weep.

Chapter 56

Jack must find Kate

William, I'm sure you realize that the woman who was riding with you is my daughter—my only child. I'm truly sorry about your friend. But right now I need to go back to where these animals left that Jeep. Maybe, just maybe, they left my daughter and the boy there. I've got to go check up on them. But I will be talking to you again. And you can count on this—I'm going to make sure we get these guys, and I will make them pay for doing this terrible thing to your friend. You've got my word on that."

Jack, still resting his hand on William's shoulder, paused a moment and then continued: "Son, are you going to be okay?"

"Mr. Handler. Larry was not just my best friend, he was my

only friend."

"I understand," Jack interrupted. "I'm going to find my daughter and the boy. And after I do, we're going after these guys. I will punish them for what they've done. It won't bring back your friend, I understand that, but that's the best I can do. Just hang in. Okay?"

William couldn't talk. But he did nod his head in agreement.

Jack patted the man on his shoulder one last time and then called to his nephew.

"Red, let's get going."

The boy had found the whole situation very unsettling. He recognized the very close relationship the two paramedics shared, and he understood that William was in deep mourning.

Red had hung on to Kate's cell phone. When his uncle called him, he immediately sent Jack a text message: "Unk Jack. Take William with us????"

"No. He needs to stay here with his friend until the police secure this crime scene. But we do need to get going," Jack declared as the two of them jumped into his vehicle.

"Buckle up, kid, and keep that cell phone handy. I've got some questions to ask you."

Chapter 57

Jack grills Red

Jack's countenance changed immediately and dramatically. No longer was he the consoling fatherly figure—his mission was changing. Red barely had time to tighten his seatbelt before Jack began vaulting his SUV over nature-strewn tree limbs and small stumps dominating the side of the dirt road. There was no time for maneuvering an elegant turnaround, so Jack had just shot through the woods for more than a hundred feet before reemerging on the narrow road.

"Do you remember how many men there were?" Jack asked Red, even while he was still dodging trees.

Red had dropped Kate's cell phone trying to keep his face from smashing into the dash.

As he bent over to pick it up, Jack barked, "Just show me fingers."

Red held up three fingers.

"That's what William thought as well. So, we're dealing with three men. Did they keep their masks on the whole time? Jack immediately rephrased his question: "Did you at any time get a look at their faces?"

Red shook his head indicating no.

"Were they dressed like other people who live around here?"

Red started shaking his head and began fingering the cell phone.

Jack saw that Red wanted to elaborate, so he did not interrupt.

As they arrived at the main road Jack shoved the shifter into park and jumped out and began dragging a few small limbs to the shoulder to mark the drive for the sheriff.

When he got back in, there was a text waiting for him.

"Well dressed. One had suit. All wore gloves."

"Did you notice anything special about their shoes?"

Red texted, "$$$, black."

"Did you hear them talk?"

Red shook his head and held his thumbs down. This time his hand signal was not for emphasis.

"Were they heavy? Thin? Younger? Older? Hang on, I'll ask them one at a time. Did they appear to be my age, or Kate's age?"

Red nodded his head but then held up one finger and pointed at Jack.

"One old guy, right?"

Red nodded.

Then Red signaled for Jack to stop, and he started fingering the phone.

Jack waited for the text.

"1 fat. Real fat."

"Okay. That helps," Jack said. "Was this fat guy the older one?"

Red shook his head.

"Here we are. This is where they ditched the Jeep."

Chapter 58

Jack warns Red

O kay, Red. I'm not sure what to expect back here. So I want you to stay in the vehicle until I say it's safe to get out. Got that?"

Red nodded.

Jack had already decided not to mark this drive for the sheriff. He made that call for two reasons.

First of all, he did not want to confuse the issue. It was critical, he believed, for the county to find and secure the other crime scene and to take care of William. Were he to have marked this road as well, the car the sheriff was sending might mistake the locations.

But, there was a second, even more compelling reason for his desire to be left alone at this point.

He believed that there was an outside chance he might encounter one of the kidnappers back there. And if that were the case, Jack wanted to be able to conduct his own interrogation—one without Miranda constraints.

Red watched Jack as he removed his revolver from his holster and placed it on the seat between his legs.

Jack had no idea what he might encounter at the end of the dirt road. He had given it considerable thought and determined that the kidnappers would not choose to ditch their vehicle at a location where they had been holed up. So, while there might be a hunting cottage back there, it wouldn't be their hideout.

No, Jack reasoned. *There's almost no chance that any of kidnappers remained behind. And it is also highly unlikely that I'm going to find Kate or the boy back here. But you just never know what you might find.*

Chapter 59

Step by step

J ack suspected that the three men might have driven the Jeep well off the dirt road to conceal it. So, he concentrated more on tracks in the loose dirt. Surmising that they would not have wanted to drive the Buick too far into the woods, Jack watched for a place where they could get a front-wheel drive sedan safely turned around.

Only a hundred yards from the main road, he found what he was looking for. Jack jumped out to examine the tracks more carefully. He could see where they had backed the Buick up off the road and turned it around.

He also spotted Jeep tracks heading off into the woods.

"Okay," Jack muttered to himself. "Let's see which way Kate and the boy went."

Jack sought to determine whether Kate and Robby had been transferred to the Buick or left with the Jeep.

It took him only a few seconds to find Kate's shoe prints crossing the road in the direction of the Buick. But no sign of Robby.

"Must be one of the men carried the boy," Jack surmised.

So far the news was encouraging: Kate was still alive, and there was no reason to think anything bad had yet happened to the boy.

With his eyes, Jack followed the ruts dug in the soil where the Jeep sped off. Quickly he slid back behind the wheel and slammed the shifter into drive.

Chapter 60

Red has Jack's back

Realizing that he could not leave Red this close to potential danger, he stopped and backed up a safe distance, still not leaving his vehicle close enough to the main road to be spotted.

"Okay, Red. See that large oak tree over there?" Jack said, pointing in the opposite direction from where the Jeep had been driven.

"I want you to take the cell phone and go over there and sit. If anyone comes up the drive, I want you to text me."

Aside from Jack's stated reason for so stationing his nephew, he was appropriately uncertain as to what he might find in the woods. And Red, he believed, had already seen enough violence for this day.

Jack took a long look around his vehicle as he waited for Red to reach the tree. Jack then called Red on his cell to be sure it was working.

"Go ahead and take a leak, and then sit down facing this way."

Even though his most recent actions had been so totally involved in catching up with the kidnappers, all the time Jack's mind was totally engaged with possible motives and intents. If he could figure those out, maybe he could predict their next move.

Jack glanced back once more to check on Red. The boy was now sitting at the base of the tree, facing him.

Jack retrieved a roll of yellow crime scene tape and then headed in the direction the Jeep tracks indicated.

Chapter 61

Detective work can be a nasty job

The Jeep tracks were distinct—no effort had been made to conceal them.

They're not worried about our finding this vehicle, Jack determined. *That means they've probably sanitized it. But they were in a hurry. People overlook things when they are in a hurry. I might just get lucky.*

Jack had walked well over fifty yards into the woods but still not had not found the Jeep.

Finally, just as he crested a large hill, he spotted it. There it was, halfway down the other side, resting against a tree, with wheels pointed upward.

It was a cinch that no one intentionally rode the Jeep down the hill, Jack surmised. *That means the driver would have got out here, put the jeep in neutral, and then released the brake.*

"Right here is where they wiped it down," he said aloud, as he began to examine the ground. "That fat driver would not have fought this hill. He would have removed everything that could tie him or his buddies to the vehicle, and then he would have released the brakes."

Jack began combing every inch of the area around where the Jeep had been parked. He immediately spotted a patch of disturbed leaves right where he suspected the driver stepped out of the vehicle.

The closer he looked, the clearer it became. The driver had gotten out, bent down and searched under and behind the front seat.

Next he had done the same around the rear seats.

Jack walked to where the back of the Jeep would have been and then around to the passenger side.

If Kate left anything for me to find, she would have concealed it well, Jack reasoned. *The fat man would not have found it.*

That was not a particularly pleasant thought for Jack because it meant that he was going to have to fight the hill himself—not something he looked forward to.

Before he checked out the Jeep, Jack decided to expand his perimeter at the top of the hill.

He was methodical. His first move was to pace off four large steps to the side and then to walk slowly in a circle around the point where the driver had searched the Jeep.

When finished with that, he paced off another four steps and repeated the effort.

On his fifth trip around the site, he noticed a piece of white paper lying about fifty feet from where the Jeep had been searched.

"Could this possibly be?" Jack asked himself out loud.

When he reached the piece of paper, he could not help himself. He burst out laughing.

"The fat man couldn't hold it," he said.

There, right next to a large maple tree, Jack saw an unusually large mound of freshly deposited excrement. And alongside it—the piece of white paper that had originally attracted his attention. It was obviously what the driver had used to clean himself.

Jack slipped on a pair of latex gloves and knelt over the evidence.

Taking a stick of wood and breaking it in half, he opened up the paper to see what was printed on it.

Chapter 62

Jack's first real clue

The first thing that Jack could make out as he spread it out on the ground were these words: "LUMBERJACK BREAKFAST."

Beneath that was a promotion of an all-you-can-eat lumberjack breakfast for seven dollars. Barely discernable beneath that was the date—between nine and eleven a.m. on the following Saturday.

"Oh my god!" Jack said, "I know exactly where the fat man wants to be Saturday morning."

Jack also made a second assumption based on the museum flier. Because the Tahquamenon Logging Museum is located just outside of Newberry, it would be likely that the men are holed up west of where Jack had found the Jeep—possibly quite close to that town. Jack realized that was just a guess, but it was at least something to consider.

Understandably excited about this find, Jack was already constructing various scenarios as to how he would deal with it. While nothing would give him more instant gratification than to beat the fat man senseless, he knew that would have to wait. Jack's first priority was to find Kate and the boy—beyond that, nothing else mattered.

Jack dropped the two sticks next to the piece of paper. He then rolled out about twenty feet of the crime scene tape and fed it around the tree. Instead of encircling it a single time, he made two wrappings and then tied the ends in a large bow.

After he had finished, he turned and headed back to where the Jeep had been parked.

However, after taking only a few steps, he had a second thought.

If Sheriff Green reaches the same conclusion as did he, deputies will stake out the Saturday breakfast. Most likely the fat man, and perhaps one of his buddies, will be apprehended. But that would not necessarily lead to Kate and Robby.

Jack concluded that his best chance to free his daughter would be to follow the fat man back to where Kate was being held.

So, Jack returned to the tree and removed the tape. He refused to destroy evidence, but he didn't feel it necessary to do the sheriff's job for him.

"Now the fun part," Jack muttered as he prepared to tackle the hill.

Chapter 63

The second clue—not enough

*A*t least it's not on its side, Jack thought. *I hate climbing through from on top.*

Getting to the Jeep was not as difficult as it might have been. Jack was able to proceed all the way down the hill without falling or otherwise using his hands.

Jack concluded from the scrapes and dents that the Jeep had rolled several times. And because the fat man had left the driver's side open when he released the brake, that door was entirely ripped off.

When he reached the vehicle, Jack checked for leaking gasoline. He smelled none. That meant the tank had not ruptured in the crash.

He then confirmed his suspicion that the license plate would be removed.

He suspected the vehicle registration and proof of insurance would also be missing, so he took a moment to write down the VIN. Even though he was certain the Jeep had been stolen, having the vehicle identification number could help him track down its origin and perhaps provide a clue as to the general location of where the kidnappers might be holding Kate and Robby.

Making sure that his inspecting the Jeep would not cause it to break loose and continue down the hill, Jack then crawled into the gaping hole on the driver's side.

Wonder what this bumpy ride might have shaken loose, Jack thought.

All he found on the roof in the front were two tubes of lip moisturizer, a handful of loose change, and a few receipts. He checked the receipts and found none dated recently. He tossed them back for the sheriff to find.

Turning to the rear of the vehicle, Jack's luck improved. Jack spotted a bright metal object. It was a New York City detective's badge.

"Okay," Jack said aloud. "Kitty made it this far."

Jack concluded that his daughter had removed her badge when still in the ambulance. Not wanting her captors to know she was a cop, and knowing that her bag would be searched, she must have hidden the badge somewhere on her person.

And then, after being forced into the Jeep, she carefully retrieved the badge from where ever she had hidden it and slid it between the seats.

Finally, when the Jeep careened onto its top and slammed against the tree, the badge became dislodged.

Kate could not have predicted all that was to transpire, but she knew that eventually Jack would search the Jeep and find it.

With a sigh of satisfaction, Jack removed the badge and slipped it into his pocket.

No need to tell the sheriff about this—this is personal property, Jack reasoned.

Jack was beginning to get a feel as to how this went down.

The three men in the Jeep forced the ambulance to a stop and then stormed it. The fat driver remained in the Jeep.

Once they had commandeered the ambulance, they immediately drove it down the dirt two-track to a point not visible from the road. There they gagged and taped the two medical technicians and Red.

Jack was quite certain that they never intended to murder anyone during this abduction. But intentions were not important at this point. The assault and imprisonment were both felonies. The fact that someone died during the commission of those felonies made all the perpetrators guilty of felony murder.

The felony murder part was a piece of information Jack was not eager for them to learn. Because, if they found out that they could be tried for murder it would make them less likely to surrender Kate and Robby under any circumstance.

The discovery of the badge told Jack one more thing.

Chapter 64

The badge talks to Jack

Kate was kidnaped for a purpose. The fact that she was able to hide her badge for Jack to find strongly suggested that her hands were not secured as were those of the other victims. Kate was kidnaped so that she could take care of Robby.

That was both good and bad news, in Jack's eyes. While Jack did not yet have any idea as to what the men wanted with the boy, he feared that once they did get what they were after, they might just dispose of both Robby and Kate.

He had to get to them quickly.

Unfortunately, Sheriff Green had made it very clear the odds were good the kidnappers had successfully eluded his roadblocks.

The sheriff then explained that while he intended to maintain the checkpoints, all parties were pretty certain that the Buick had turned off Highway M-28 somewhere west of M-123 but east of Newberry. That was good news, in that it supported Jack's suspicion that he should turn his attention to the Newberry area.

Jack recognized the fact that there were not enough officers in the UP to search every hunting and fishing cottage in Chippewa and Luce counties.

Even though he was confident that the sheriff would do all in his power to round up the kidnappers and rescue Kate and Robby, Jack was convinced that the best chance for success resided in his own suspicion that Kate and Robby were being held in the vicinity of Newberry. Jack intended to concentrate his efforts there. But, if he were unable to locate them by Saturday morning, Jack believed that the fat man would not miss his opportunity for a cheap all-you-can-eat lumberjack breakfast, so that's where he would be as well.

Jack felt that while Sheriff Green had good intentions, he still was essentially a rookie at his job—to him the book contained the rules you followed, not something you throw at the "scumbags."

Jack practiced a very different crime solving method. While he had no interest in strong-arming the wrong guy, he was much bigger on coercing than reading Mirandas.

Gripping Kate's badge tightly, Jack resolved himself to do whatever was necessary to get her back—with or without the sheriff's blessing or help.

Chapter 65

The breakfast

As Jack prepared to make his way back toward his vehicle, he began playing back his recollections about the Tahquamenon Logging Museum breakfasts—he had actually attended one a few years earlier.

He was in the UP with three friends for a fishing trip, and one of his fishing buddies suggested that they see what the Lumberjack Breakfast was all about. He recalled that he was quite impressed with the authentic nature of the event.

The breakfasts were indeed "all you can eat," prepared on wood-fired stoves.

People were seated on benches arranged on both sides of twelve-foot tables covered with blue and white checkered tablecloths.

The waiting line stretched from the serving area at the front of the shack, all the way outside, and then some.

Jack could picture the fat man waiting impatiently in that line to get his serving of pancakes, bacon, eggs, toast, orange juice and coffee.

Today was Friday.

That meant that Jack would have to wait only a few hours before springing his trap.

Jack hoped that he would not have to wait until tomorrow. It would not be easy to take the fat man down in a crowded venue such as that. But if all else failed, that remained an option.

Determined that he was finished with the Jeep, Jack attacked the hill. Climbing to the top required more exertion than did the trip down, but it was easier in that he could use his hands for balance.

Strange as it might seem, Jack thought, *I don't think these guys had anything to do with the bombing. They are intent on saving the boy, for whatever reasons, not killing him.*

Just as he crested it—but before he was able to catch his breath— his cell vibrated.

Chapter 66

Jack bends the truth

Jack checked the display. It was a text from Red: "Cop car."

Jack immediately called the boy and said, "Red, sit tight. I'll be right there."

By the time Jack had made it back to where his vehicle was parked, Sheriff Green had pulled in behind him.

"Any luck, Sheriff?"

"No. We pulled off the roadblocks. They must have taken a side road. Or maybe shot up north of here. How about you? Did you find anything?"

"Down there a hundred yards or so," Jack said, pointing in the direction from which he had just come. "I marked it, where they pushed the Jeep over the hill."

"Really? Find anything of interest?"

"No. I did poke around a little. But it looks like they sanitized it pretty good. I wore gloves, so I didn't mess it up. But, on the surface at least, it appears clean."

"I'll get my technicians over here and run it."

"You might want to hit the ambulance first. One of the paramedics didn't make it."

"I found your markings. I've got a crew there right now. William, the surviving technician, told me the redheaded kid was fine, and that you took him with you. So, where is he?"

Jack pointed over toward Red and motioned for him to join them.

Sheriff Green looked at the boy, who had already risen to his feet, and then spoke to Jack in a commanding fashion.

"I want both of you, you and the boy, to be in my office first thing tomorrow morning for a debriefing.

"The bodies are beginning to pile up again. Be there at nine."

As the sheriff continued to talk Jack slipped his hand into his right pants pocket and gripped his daughter's badge. He did not hear a word that was said to him.

Chapter 67

And then there's pain

Kate made sure she grabbed medical supplies when she realized she was to be Robby's nurse. She sensed the gravity of the situation, for injuries as severe as the boy's, if not treated properly by professionals, could throw him into shock. That could prove fatal.

She was not pleased with their physical conditions—especially given the type of injury the boy had suffered.

The cottage was clean enough, for a cottage. But that's what it was—a fishing cottage. It was cedar sided—never sealed or painted. So the boards were weathered to an earthy gray. Windows were covered with yellowed newspapers, emitting the odor of garage sale comic books.

There was a small wood stove in the corner with a stack of dried wood just outside the door.

Inside, three of the rooms were finished off with fairly high-quality paneling—probably left over from a large building project or perhaps a fire sale. All of the floors were constructed from rough-cut one-inch boards nailed directly to the floor joists—no subflooring.

A cheap old broom stood in the corner of the living room, with a yellow plastic dustpan snapped to its handle. The furniture in the living room consisted of an old brown corduroy couch, three wooden kitchen chairs, and a vintage fifties Formica table.

Kate flicked a light switch in the kitchen.

"At least the power works," she sighed in relief.

She opened the refrigerator door. It was cold and didn't stink.

It could be worse, she reasoned. *But it is still not a safe place for a burn victim.*

As she walked around the cottage, she played back in her mind the moments before they had arrived there. She had been able to observe surroundings right up to the point the driver had turned south off of Highway M-28.

But at that point, the man sitting in the front seat ordered the man in the back with Kate and Robby to push the boy's head down between his knees. He then reached back, grabbed Kate by the hair, and shoved her face down onto her lap.

"Try to raise your head, little lady, and I'll break your neck right here. And then you won't be able to take care of the kid."

Chapter 68

Kate plots her escape

For a short moment, Kate thought of grabbing the man's hand and separating his fingers. The pain she could exact would be so intense that he would be forced to use his free hand to ward her off.

She then could release the man's hand and use the leverage of the seat to break his neck.

But then she would be left with the other two.

Kate was quite sure the overweight driver was not armed—he just didn't seem the type. She regarded him as dull-witted and slow to react. Besides, he was engaged in driving the car.

Her attention flashed back to the man in front of her.

If I snap his neck, I can reach into his holster and grab his gun, she was thinking. *But is the safety on or off? Is it strapped in the holster? These guys do not strike me as seasoned pros. So the 9mm might be strapped and snapped.*

And I'm not sure about the man dealing with Robby. He takes orders from the man in front. He is right handed—I could tell that by the way he grabbed Robby's head. And I'm not sure if he's armed. If I killed the man in front, I would catch the fellow holding Robby by surprise, but just for a moment. If he grabbed for me, I could elbow his nose and knock him off. But what if he used Robby as a shield or tried to strangle him? It could take me a few seconds to acquire and engage the firearm. By then Robby could be seriously hurt or even killed.

And if the driver were distracted, he could run the car into a tree.

The numbers are not right. Too many things I don't know. This is not my opportunity. Not yet.

All of these thoughts raced through Kate's mind as she sat in the back with her face smashed tightly against her knees by the heavy hand of the man in front.

Instead of taking action at this time, she counted off the minutes and seconds after turning south off M-28.

Good road, she determined. *Not especially bumpy. And quite straight. Five forty. Five fifty.*

We're turning left. Ten. Fifteen. Twenty. Thirty. Forty. A minute ten. Thirty. Two minutes. Three minutes. Four minutes. Now we're turning right. Still a good road. Ten. Fifteen. Twenty. Kate continued to count.

"We should have stopped and picked up some eggs and—" The driver started to say before he was interrupted.

"Shut up! Just shut up," the man in the front barked.

"But we don't have anything to cook for breakfast tomorrow—"

"Shut the hell up!"

Two ten. Two twenty. Kate maintained her silent counting.

The car then turned to the left—down a drive that was substantially more bouncy. Kate started her counting over.

Ten. Twenty. Thirty. Forty.

"Turn here," the man said.

"But the cottage is over there—"

"Would you just shut up and do what I tell you!"

"Oh, I get it—"

"Would you shut the hell up! That's it, freak. Open your mouth again before we get there, and I'll ram this down your throat," he said, spreading his jacket open with his free hand to show the fat man his holstered 9mm.

The man was still holding Kate down with his left hand. As he yelled at the driver, his hand pushed down harder and harder on the back of her head.

"Where did you find this imbecile?" he said, throwing back an angry glare at the man in the back. But the man in the backseat did not look at him or respond.

"Just do what I say, and keep your mouth shut," he commanded.

He then took his pistol out of his shoulder holster and pointed it at the driver's head.

"Open your mouth one more time and it'll be your last."

Okay, Kate calculated. *That would have been Quarry Road we turned south on. Had to have been. Then after about five miles we turned east for maybe a mile. And then back south for a couple miles. Maybe a bit more. And then off the main road to the east. Can't tell much after that. I should be able to retrace and find this place.*

"Okay, sweetheart," the boss said as he pulled Kate's head up so she could look him in the eyes.

Chapter 69

These guys are not pros

P ressing the gun to her forehead while still clutching her hair, he continued: "You are alive. You should be happy about that. Just keep this in mind—I don't need you. You're useful to me only to take care of the boy. Nothing else. Remember that."

"Yes sir," she submissively responded, affecting fear.

Taurus 9mm. Not a Glock," she observed. *Safety on. Finger on trigger. These guys are very dangerous, but definitely not pros.*

Kate was able to deduce that because all 9mm semi-automatic pistols are less reliable than a quality revolver. Plus, a semi-auto indiscriminately discharges the spent rounds, while the revolver stores them in the cylinder for removal later. Professionals know spent rounds deposited at the scene of a crime are evidence.

She could determine from the type of gun he was brandishing that her captors were deadly, but they were not professional killers.

Before she allowed the men to place Robby in a bed, she searched through the closet until she found some clean sheets.

The men objected.

"You don't understand," she said. "This boy has some very serious burns. If infection sets in, he will not be able to think or speak coherently. And he could die."

Chapter 70

Kate spots her opportunity

L ittle by little, Robby was weaving together the words he overheard with what he already knew.

"Kate, what's this all about?" he pleaded.

"Robby, these men think you have information about something your dad found on the sunken ship ... and where he might have hidden it. Do you know *anything* about that?"

"I'm cold. Can I have another blanket?"

"Sure, hon. I'll find you one."

Kate walked out of Robby's bedroom and into the master bedroom. "The boy needs another blanket," she said loudly as she hurried past her captors.

From the closet she scooped up several blankets off a shelf.

As she tucked them under her arm, she glanced down and saw a shiny metal object protruding from the top of an ankle-high hiking boot.

She reached down with her left hand and pulled it out.

A jackknife, she said to herself. *What fishing cottage wouldn't have one of these laying around?*

She set the blankets down on the floor, opened the yellow knife, and felt the blade.

Sharp, very sharp, she observed.

Leaving the knife open, she slid it blade up into her right-side jacket pocket, picked up the blankets, and returned to Robby.

"Here you go. Maybe these will help," she said, placing her hand on his hot forehead.

"I'm going to get you a cold glass of water. Could you use some water?"

"Thanks, but I'm too cold. I just want to see my mom. Why won't they let me see my mom?"

Kate remembered that she had an unopened bottle of water in her jacket pocket. She unscrewed the top, and said, "I'll talk to the men. But for right now I would like you to try to drink this water. I think you have a little fever, and the water will help."

"I'll try. Where's Red? I'd like to see Red."

"Red's with his uncle, my father. They'll get here as soon as they can. But for right now, you should drink some water. And I'll talk to the men. Okay, kiddo?"

Kate knew time was getting short. Robby had a bad fever. He could go into shock. And that could kill him.

The kidnappers had disconnected the intravenous line when they pulled Kate and Robby from the ambulance. Kate knew dehydration was also a possibility.

"Gotta find a way outta here!" She mumbled to herself. "This kid can't wait until morning."

"Did he tell you anything?" the boss asked as she walked out into the living room. "The sooner I find out what I want to know, the sooner I can let you two go."

Kate, knowing that the men never intended to free them, hatched a plan on the fly.

"Robby is sleeping now, but he did tell me something. Might be what you're looking for."

"What did he say?" the boss demanded.

Chapter 71

Kate plots to divide and conquer

Robby said that he and his father went to the State Harbor Park, just off Whitefish Point Road near the Shipwreck Museum. At night. And that his dad made several trips with a red hand truck. They parked in the lot, and Robby walked out on the pier. And his dad took something out of the back of their vehicle and moved it into a rusty old boat south of the harbor."

"Was the boat in the water?"

"No, it was just pulled up on land and on blocks. I've seen it there. It's ancient. Hasn't been in the water for decades."

"Several trips with a hand truck?"

"That's what he said. I think that's the old fish-smoking plant … or something like that. It's posted."

"You lying to me?"

"Look, you told me to ask Robby some questions. I did, and that's what he told me. I don't know what his father was hiding in that old boat, and neither does Robby."

"Why would he ever pick a place like that?"

"Why wouldn't he?" Kate quickly countered. "It's posted with a "Keep Out" sign. Sounds to me like a pretty good hiding spot. No one ever goes by that old boat."

"We're going to check it out. If we find what we're looking for, when I come back, you can take the boy to a hospital. If I don't find it, then I'm not going to be very happy. And I will make damn sure that you're not going to be very happy either."

Kate knew that if she and Robby were around when the boss came back, they'd both be dead.

Her plan was simple. Coax one or two of the men out of the cottage—that would even the odds a little.

"Sit down in this chair," the boss said, grabbing her by the arm and slamming her down hard into a rustic wooden dining room chair.

"Put your hands behind you."

Just as she had anticipated, she was about to be tied up. That meant that the boss was himself going to check out the State Harbor boat. He didn't trust his men enough to dispatch them to retrieve the loot—whatever it was.

"Here," the boss said, handing a role of gray duct tape to the fat man. "Tape her hands behind her, and then tape them to the back of the chair as well. Use a lot of tape, make sure she can't slip out of it."

Chapter 72

Kate is a cop, after all

When the fat man was finished, the boss checked his work.

"That should do the trick," he said.

"Sorry to have to do this to you, sweetheart. But I wouldn't want to have you do something stupid."

So far this was just as Kate envisioned it. The fat man and the boss were going to go to the bogus hiding spot. And she would be left alone with Quietman and, of course, Robby.

It will take them nearly a hour to get there, Kate reasoned. *They will spend at least half an hour searching the boat. And then another hour to get home. So, once they leave this cottage, I have two and a half hours to work with. Won't even have to rush it.*

"Let me see your gun," the boss said to Quietman. "You ever shot that thing?" he asked, as Quietman awkwardly pulled his 9mm half out of his holster.

"I know how to use it," he replied, sliding it back and strapping it in.

Kate observed that it was identical to the boss's gun.

"The girl is taped to the chair," the boss said. "I checked—she's secure. All you have to do is make sure she stays there. Don't open the door for anyone. We'll be back in a couple hours—maybe less. There's some food in the fridge if you get hungry."

The fat man was unhappy. "Do we pass any grocery stores?" he asked.

"Food!" the boss exclaimed. "You're always worried about where your next meal will come from."

"I'm just sayin'," he protested, "people gotta eat. And I know *exactly* where my next meal's coming from. I'm gonna hit that big breakfast at the Lumberjack Museum in the morning. It's 'all you can eat.' Believe me—I understand what *that* means."

The boss rolled his eyes and yelled back at Quietman just before he closed the door: "We're taking the Rover. They might be looking for the Buick."

So, Kate thought, *the Buick is just outside the door, with the keys in it. And I've got a couple hours.*

Quietman walked around behind Kate and tested the tautness of the duct tape for himself—but said nothing.

He then returned to an old but comfortable leather recliner and fingered through some regional books and magazines that were lying on a glass-topped table beside the chair. While not facing

Kate exactly, he could still catch her out of the corner of his eye.

Now I wished I'd put the knife in my pocket pointed down. This could be tricky, Kate thought.

Chapter 73

Duct tape—strength or weakness?

While her wrists were securely taped together, there was only a small amount of the sticky side wrapped around the dowel rod on the back of the chair.

Maybe I can get this tape to let loose from the chair, and then I could slide my hands up and down, she thought.

As she pulled upward in her attempt to break the tape loose, the unexpected happened. The dowel actually pulled out of the seat.

Kate felt and heard it give but wasn't quite sure what had happened.

Even though the sound was not substantial, Quietman also heard it. He glanced over at Kate.

She immediately stretched out both legs, changing her weight distribution on the chair, and causing a similar clicking sound.

Quietman pulled the Taurus 9mm out of his holster, laid it on the table beside him, and then returned to his reading.

Kate then began moving her hands from side to side while pulling downward, trying to dislodge the dowel from the top of the chair back.

The longer she worked at it, the looser it became. Finally, she sensed that it was offering very little resistance.

She slowed her movements down, so when it gave, it would do so as quietly as possible.

Kate could tell when it finally let loose. She drew her hands back against the chair and rested.

No need to move too quickly. Could get careless.

Then sliding her fingers into the space now open on the back of the chair, she gathered a small section of her jacket and pulled it to the left.

Little by little the knife-side pocket slid closer to where she could access it.

She looked over at Quietman. His head was beginning to nod up and down—he was falling asleep.

That was both good and bad news for Kate.

Chapter 74

Quietman grows more quiet

While his erratic slumber would dull his senses, she knew that as soon as he realized what he was doing, he would come back and check to be sure her hands were still secured to the chair.

She now had to work quickly.

I'm close, she said to herself. *Just have to get to that pocket and the knife.*

Kate soon learned just how difficult that would be.

Getting the jacket pulled around so she could reach it was one thing—retrieving the knife was another.

As she pulled it out of her pocket, she failed to get a secure grip on it, and it tumbled to the floor behind her.

Fortunately, it landed point down, and it stuck.

While the noise that it made was minimal, it was enough to awaken Quietman.

His head snapped up.

"Did you hear that?" she inquired loudly. "Robby's awake. I need to check on him. Untie me!"

"*I'll* check it out," Quietman responded.

As soon as Quietman entered Robby's room, Kate stood to her feet and lunged toward the gun on the table.

Bending down and reaching behind her, she fumbled with it until she was able to switch the safety off.

Not sure if Quietman's pistol had a round in the chamber, Kate pulled back the slide to engage one.

"Oh my god!" she exclaimed.

The slide had stuck on the magazine. Not only was there no round in the chamber—the magazine was empty as well.

"This gun is empty!" she muttered.

As quickly as she could, she returned the pistol to the table and ran back toward the chair. But before she slid her arms over the back, she reached down and picked up the knife.

No time to cut the tape. Must come up with a plan B.

Chapter 75

Blood starved

Quietman walked back out of Robby's bedroom and squeezed the door closed behind him.

"The boy's sound asleep," he said with a suspicious look on his face.

He looked down at the table and saw the pistol was not as he had left it.

Quietman then looked over at Kate. He stood there for a moment thinking.

Kate stared into his eyes, begging him to investigate.

He complied.

Sliding between the table and recliner, he rapidly approached her.

Kate used his momentum.

As he neared her, she stiffly kicked his knee, causing him to fall to her left.

She stood, knife pointing downward behind her, and fell on him as he turned to get up.

Kate aimed the knife at his groin—more specifically, at his right femoral artery.

She knew she was cutting his flesh, but she was not sure she had hit the artery until hot blood spurted onto her hands.

Quietman said nothing as he grabbed her neck and began choking her.

Kate sensed she was not getting blood to her brain and knew she would soon black out. But she kept stabbing at his crotch. Once she was certain she had adequately sliced up his right femoral, she rolled slightly to her right, pulled the blade back a bit and attacked his left artery.

It would only be a matter of time before he bled out or she passed out.

When Quietman realized what she was up to, he immediately ceased choking her and used his last strength to roll her off to the side. He lifted his head high enough to see the yellow-handled fishing knife protruding from his crotch and tried to pull it out, but he was unable to close his fingers around it. He was in the last stage of dying.

Kate, already unconscious from lack of blood to her brain, lay face down and helpless on the floor right beside the man she was killing.

There is a short period of time—usually about a minute—between the point a person passes out from strangulation and when death, or at least permanent brain damage, occurs. Kate had almost reached that stage of limbo. She was out, and fresh blood had not yet begun circulating to her brain.

Chapter 76

The sticky pool

As she slowly regained awareness of her surroundings, she suddenly remembered how she had ended up on the floor. Frantically, she forced a distance between Quietman and herself by kicking against him with her feet.

That's when she realized she was lying in a pool of Quietman's warm sticky blood. It had soaked through her clothes all the way to her skin.

At first she gagged at the thought and smell of all that blood, but she then realized she must act quickly.

Kate spun her body around so that she could pull the knife from Quietman's body, and then she set about cutting the duct tape from her hands.

As soon as her hands were free, she ran into the master bedroom, stripping down to her bra as she did.

She flipped open a suitcase on the bed and selected a black pullover sweater and a long sleeved shirt—both were men's size XL, and so they fit her like a tent.

Once dressed, but before she disturbed Robby, she ran out the door to confirm that the Buick was actually in the driveway. No point in waking up Robby until a method of escape had been verified.

She opened the driver's side door and slid in behind the wheel.

"The boss took the keys!"

Kate recalled that when first allowed to raise her head she spotted a large outbuilding behind and to the left side of the house.

That's plenty large enough to store a vehicle, she thought.

She ran full bore to a set of two swinging doors and looked in a small dirty window. Inside she spotted an older red Ford four-wheel drive pickup truck.

"No point hiding the keys for that antique—if it runs, the keys are in it," she actually said aloud.

Strung between two eyebolts was an extraordinarily heavy-duty welded link chain. She knew she would never be able to force the chain or the eyebolts, but the rusty padlock looked vulnerable to her.

At first she grabbed a ten-foot length of rusty one-inch black pipe. She slid it into the loop of the chain and tried to force the lock open.

"That's not going to work," she said, tossing it aside and opting for a four-inch concrete block.

Lifting the block even with her face, she brought it crashing down directly at the top of the padlock. The force of that single blow dislodged the shackle and freed the chain.

Chapter 77

It ran like a Ford

The driver's side door was rusted and wrenched so that it would not fully close.

"That's not a good sign," she said as she jumped in.

Just as she had thought, the keys were in the ignition switch. But when she tried starting the engine, it barely clicked.

She slammed her hand hard on the steering wheel and looked to the side.

"Ah ha!" she exclaimed, spotting an eighty-amp battery charger all plugged in and ready to go.

"Looks like they've been here before."

Checking under the dash for the hood release but not finding one, she reasoned, *maybe the primary latch is already released.*

She jumped out and tried lifting the hood. It was securely closed with both latches engaged.

Kate then ran around to the driver's side and stuck her head under the dash. Finally finding the hood release, she pulled on it as hard as she could, but it did not budge.

Getting back in the seat, she gripped it with both hands and gave a mighty tug.

Clunk!

"Got it!" she exclaimed.

She jumped back out and fingered the secondary latch.

"Let's see, this is pretty dirty, but positive is always red."

She attached the charger to the battery and turned it to a full eighty amps.

After giving the battery a moment to charge, she activated the ignition switch. All the dashboard lights came on.

"Now that's good sign!" she said. "Let's see if it starts."

It was amazing. The engine barely turned over once before it fired up.

"Wow, look at this baby smoke!" she said as she removed the charger and dropped the hood.

When she put the shifter in reverse, the truck did not move for over a second. And when it did try to engage, the engine dogged down and almost died.

Kate then stepped hard on the gas to prevent the engine from dying. This caused both rear wheels to spin as the truck lunged back through the open double doors.

It was a V-8 engine, and it was firing on all eight. And, it appeared to be running fine.

"Gas?" she questioned.

Looking down at the gauge, she confirmed that there was gas in the tank—it was more than half full.

Kate slammed the door closed, but it didn't latch. Looking behind her she spotted a black bungee cord attached behind her seat. She pulled it taut and hooked it through the slightly opened window.

"That's how they do it," she said.

As she turned the truck around, she reached down to find the headlight switch. But before she could turn them on, she was shocked by what she saw.

Chapter 78

They've got him!

The light in Robby's room had been turned on.

Her eyes then caught movement in front and slightly to the right of her—the taillights of the Rover speeding down the driveway toward the road.

"Oh my god! The boy!" she shouted.

Kate hit the gas and spun the wheels all the way to the front door.

When she tried to shove the door open, the bungee cord snapped it back. She unhooked it and raced through the open door.

"They've got him! They've taken Robby!" Kate yelled as she ran into the boy's room.

Quietman was just as she had left him. But his blood was

tracked around the cottage. Kate grabbed the 9mm from the table and began to look for ammunition.

"Could it be?" she mumbled, as she knelt beside the dead man and searched through his pockets.

Sure enough. In his right blood-soaked pants pocket, she felt them—a substantial number of cold aluminum rounds. She grabbed as many as she could wrap her fingers around and pulled them out.

Eight, nine, ten. That's plenty.

Taking her find over to the kitchen sink, she closed off the drain and dropped them loudly into the stainless steel sink.

Gotta get all the blood off of them, or they'll gum up the gun, she was thinking as she turned the water on. *Sure hope they're sealed.*

The rounds looked to be new, so she felt comfortable running water over them.

She then placed the cleaned bullets on a towel and dried them with a second towel.

"That'll do it," she said, finding a can of WD-40 and spraying them.

She removed the excess lubricant with a third towel, and then loaded all ten rounds into the magazine.

Before she inserted the clip, she sprayed some WD-40 into the action and down the barrel.

Then, after inserting the magazine, she pulled the slide back and released it, snapping a round into the chamber. She then engaged the safety.

"This should be good to go," she said.

But before she ran out of the door, Kate returned to Quietman's body and removed his blood-covered cell phone.

Kate had no idea why the boss and the fat man had returned.

She was just thankful that she had been able to free herself so quickly.

They must have thought I'd escaped into the woods, she thought as she examined the cell phone.

It's off—must be no service at the cottage.

She turned it on and flipped it onto the seat beside her and then hit the gas.

Chapter 79

Setting the trap

They don't know this truck," she said out loud. "If I don't get too close I should be able to tail them."

Red checked the incoming text on Kate's phone: "Unk Jack wth you?"

Red shoved the cell in Jack's face. Jack had finally managed to pry Sheriff Green off his back.

As soon as Jack saw it was Kate, he locked the brakes and pulled to the side of the road. Jack was already headed south on M-123—approaching the M-28 intersection. His intention was to go west on M-28 toward Newberry. Because of the flier he had discovered near the ditched Jeep, he strongly suspected that Robby and Kate were being held in that area.

"Where are U?" Jack texted after he grabbed the cell from Red's hand.

Kate recognized her father's abruptness and called him.

"Dad—they've got Robby."

"You okay?"

"I am. But they're driving a Range Rover now. I'm right behind them in a red Ford pickup. We're on M-28, just east of Newberry—headed west."

"I suspected as much—I'm on my way there now. How many of them are there? Still three?"

"Two. One of them didn't make it."

"But you're okay?"

"Fine. But I'm worried about Robby. He needs a hospital."

"How far west of 123 are you, and how fast are you driving?"

Jack was already nearing the crossroads.

"I'm guessing fifteen miles. They're driving the speed limit—55."

"That gives us enough time," Jack said, cooking up his plan on the fly. Drop back far enough so they don't make you."

"I'm good. I can watch them. And they don't know this vehicle."

"About a mile from where they intersect—123 and 28. Get in close behind them. It's a four-way stop. Box them in. I'll see what I can do to disrupt things from my end."

Kate had a lot of confidence in her father's resourcefulness. She knew without question that he'd be waiting for her and that he would have something special set up for the kidnappers.

"Whatcha got in mind?"

Chapter 80

Trap set—need cheese

W e've got a few options. They know *this* vehicle, so I'm a
bit limited in that respect. We'll just have to see what
opportunities they give us."

Jack checked Red's cell charge and then asked Kate: "How's the
battery on the cell you're using?"

"Five percent."

"Turn it off for now—save the battery. And then, if you can,
turn it back on and call me when you get within a mile of the
intersection."

"Will do," Kate said as she clicked off.

Jack considered having the sheriff set up a roadblock, but with
Robby's life on the line, he opted against an overt police presence.

Pulling back on M-123 Jack sped with earnest until they reached the M-28 intersection.

"We should beat Kate here by at least five minutes," Jack said to Red as they pulled over.

"I want you to jump out and wait over there," Jack said, pointing to a stand of evergreen trees north and west of where they'd stopped.

Red, nervously staring out of the windshield, nodded his head in agreement.

"I'm not sure exactly what will happen next, but I want you to remain behind those trees until I call you. If Kate or I *don't* call or come for you, you still stay there until at least three cop cars arrive on the scene, and you're positive that all the shooting has stopped. Got that?"

Red again nodded.

"Okay, son, take off."

Jack had pulled off on the west side of the road, right beside a double trailer log hauler. He jumped out and called over to two men standing nearby. "This rig belong to one of you?"

"Yeah. It's mine," said a tall heavy-set man wearing a soiled denim jacket. "You need me to move it?"

"No," Jack said, flashing a badge. "I want you to leave it right there. And I want the two of you to jump in your buddy's car and get the hell outta here. Right now!"

The two men looked at each other and then back at Jack.

"Didn't I make myself clear enough? Get the hell outta here!"

With that, they jumped in the car and circled south on M-123.

Jack got back in his vehicle and backed up so that he was totally concealed by the log truck.

After several minutes, Kate called: "We've had to slow down

to 45. They're right behind a double truck hauling logs. We're approaching the intersection. Can you see us?"

Jack pulled ahead just a bit to get a look at the Rover.

"I can see them … and you. Pull in tighter behind them. Don't hit them, just box them in. By any chance, are you armed?"

"Actually I am. It's a 9mm Taurus. But I'm not sure it will even work—it had a lot of blood in it. Better than nothing."

"Maybe you'd better duck down, if you're not sure about your weapon. Or at least use a lot of caution."

Jack backed up and prepared to pull onto M-123.

Just before he did, he spotted a county car approaching the intersection from the north. It was Sheriff Green's car.

"Oh my god!" Jack barked. "This is just too weird."

It was clear to Jack that the truck was going to beat Sheriff Green to the stop sign. And because the sheriff did not have his lights on, the truck would have the right of way.

As the log truck started through the intersection, Jack pulled in directly behind the sheriff and engaged his four-wheel drive. He then waited until the truck was directly in front of the sheriff's car, and then he buried his foot into the accelerator.

Even though the sheriff locked his brakes, Jack's Tahoe was easily able to push the car into the side of the log truck.

He dropped to the floor of his vehicle, feigning injury.

Chapter 81

Let the fireworks begin

The boss and the fat man were in shock. And so was the sheriff—he drew his weapon and ran back to see what Jack was up to.

The boss looked over at the fat man and commanded: "Stay put." And he stepped out of the Land Rover.

Kate carefully slipped out of the old Ford truck. This time she disconnected the bungee cord first.

Using the truck door as a partial shield, she flicked off the safety and yelled: "Get down on your belly and spread your arms out."

The boss spun around, pointing his gun at her.

Before he had a chance to even think about getting a shot off,

Kate had put three rounds into him—one through his open mouth severing his brain stem, and two more into his head as he slowly slumped to the road. His gun slid under the Land Rover. "Fatman! Get outta the car with your hands raised! Now!"

"Don't shoot! Don't shoot! I'm not armed," he yelled as he fumbled with the door.

When he finally got it opened, he sprawled out on his belly, continuing to cry out: "Don't hurt me. Please don't hurt me. They made me do this. I'm not one of them. Please don't hurt me."

At the sound of gunfire Jack jumped out of his vehicle. Pushing the sheriff to the side, he ran full speed toward the scene of the gunfire.

"Spread 'em!" Kate shouted, driving her knee into the fat man's spine.

"You're hurting me. I told you, I'm not one of them. They made me do it."

"Shut up!" Kate admonished the fat man.

"Try this on him," Jack said, extending a large nylon zip tie.

"Not too tight, please," the fat man pleaded. "I have a circulation problem. Please not too tight."

"Dad, could you take over here?" Kate requested, after securing the fat man's hands behind him. "I want to check up on Robby."

Chapter 82

Jack under arrest?

Jack had already raced around the Rover and confirmed the boss was dead. He then reached in and pulled out the man's wallet.

"He was a local. Sault Ste. Marie. His name was Ronald Lawrence Harper. Remember that name," Jack said.

Kate did not respond, nor did she even hear what her father had just said.

"Robby, how ya doin', darlin'?" Kate asked upon opening the rear door. "Are you sleeping?"

The boy wasn't sleeping. And Kate knew it. He was unconscious.

Kate felt his forehead—he was burning up.

"Dad. Could you come over here?" Kate called out.

"No, he can't," Sheriff Green, said. "Your father is under arrest."

"For what?" Jack asked.

"For half a dozen violations," the sheriff said. He had holstered his handgun but was wielding a pair of handcuffs in a menacing manner.

"Look, Sheriff. You're going to receive a commendation for this if you play your cards right."

"What're you talking about?"

"Here's how you spin it." Jack coached him. "You knew that the only way to stop the suspects without causing harm to the boy would be to create a distraction. This would allow enough time for Kate to get the drop on them. We were working together—you, Kate and me. Look, the bottom line is this: Your plan worked. You saved the boy."

The sheriff just stood there dumbfounded. Finally, he took a look into the rear of the Rover, and asked, "How's the boy?"

"He needs a hospital," Jack replied. "I'd like to move him into my vehicle and drive him into the Soo. I'm afraid we don't have time to wait for an ambulance. And it's not like that worked out so well last time."

"Where's Red?" Kate asked.

"Waiting where it's safe," Jack replied as he started to call the boy on his cell. He then thought better of it, and simply yelled in Red's direction: "Hey! Red! Get over here! Kate's worried about you."

Red let out a roar of extreme joy—loud enough for all to hear and then bolted full speed in their direction.

"There were three of these guys. Do we know where the other one is?" the sheriff asked.

"He's dead," Kate replied.

"Where's his body?"

Kate, who was still sitting in the backseat of the Rover attending Robby glanced at the dash.

"Check the GPS. Looks like they were using it."

She halted and took a closer look.

"Dad, take a look at their destination. What do you make of *that?*"

Chapter 83

Sheriff Green checks the GPS

Jack had already headed over to retrieve his vehicle for the trip to the hospital.

"Can I safely assume that the third man did not die from natural causes?" the sheriff asked.

"I killed him. The knife is still there. That's how I escaped."

Red opened the rear passenger door and immediately placed his hand on Robby's head.

Robby sensed that his friend was there, and he opened his eyes.

"Red. Is that you?" Robby asked. "I don't feel so good. I'm freezing."

Red gave Kate a questioning look.

"I know. He's burning up. It's the infection from his burns. He's got a fever, and he thinks he's cold. Uncle Jack is going to take him to the hospital. I think he wants you to ride along. Is that okay?"

Red nodded.

"Sheriff. Take a look at that destination on their GPS. What does that look like to you?"

Sheriff Green stepped over the boss's body and slid in behind the wheel. The Rover was in park but still running.

"Let's see, what do we have here? Looks like— You know what? That looks like the missing guy … *this* boy's parents. That looks like his property. Why would they be headed to the Gordon house?"

"They were looking for something but were not quite sure what it was. But they seemed to think that Robby might have seen his father hide something. I would assume it's something of substantial value—for all this trouble, it would have to be. They were trying to get Robby to give them some information."

"Do you suppose the boy told them anything?"

"He might have. But I don't think he knows anything."

Kate thought about it a moment and then spoke: "I had sent them to State Harbor, near Whitefish Point. I told them that Robby had said he saw his father hide something in the large old boat there. I wanted to improve my odds by getting one or two of them out of the house. That's how I escaped."

"Must be the boss got a call from someone, giving him different information. Probably relating to the Gordon property.

"Or, maybe the boss decided he'd rather have Robby with him when he went to State Harbor, and so he came back for the boy. And then, when the boss asked him about State Harbor, and Robby didn't know what he was talking about, the boss realized it was all a lie. So he decided to check out the Gordon house. But that's all just conjecture. You might want to check the boss' cell, see who called him last."

Jack had returned with his vehicle and parked it a few feet from where the fat man lie cuffed on the pavement.

As he approached the Rover to transfer Robby, he glanced down and observed that the fat man's tongue was hanging out of his open mouth. His eyes were open and appeared fully dilated.

"The bastard's dead," Jack muttered too low to be heard. "I'll bet the fat old fart had a heart attack. The sheriff's not going to be very happy about that."

"Need help with Robby?" Kate asked.

"I'll pick him up. When I do, you move his blankets into my backseat. We really need to get him some attention—this kid's burning up. Red, I want you ride in back with your friend."

Kate sat in the front passenger seat. As soon as they got Robby situated, Jack backed up and turned his vehicle around.

"Hey, Sheriff. I think our fat friend here crapped his pants. You might want to attend to him."

Chapter 84

Jack tries to piece story together

Not waiting around for the sheriff to comment, Jack shoved the shifter into drive and sank his foot into the gas.

"What was that all about—the bit about the fat man crapping his pants?" Kate asked.

"The fat man must have had a heart attack. He's dead."

"Now that's a shame. I would really have liked to ask him a few questions. Do you suppose I killed him when I cuffed him?"

"You didn't do it. I'd say he just didn't have the right constitution for this type of work.

"The sheriff's pretty savvy," Jack said, trying to reassure his daughter that she was not responsible for the fat man's death. "He'll loosen his hands and roll him over on his back before the medical examiner gets there. But rest assured—your cuffing him had nothing to do with it. He was death waiting to happen. Too many French fries."

Kate turned in her seat and took a close look at Robby.

"Can we go a little faster?"

"Open the glove box," Jack told her.

Kate released the latch and pulled out a red magnetic emergency flasher. She plugged it into the cigarette lighter and handed it flashing to her father.

"Now we can," Jack said, reaching out the window attaching it to the roof.

Only a few seconds passed before Kate asked: "You got this figured out?"

"No."

"Neither do I," Kate replied. "But I do think that there are several different dynamics at play here. What do you think?"

"At least a couple," Jack agreed. "These two, three if you count the dead guy at the cottage where they held you and Robby, they had nothing to do with the three fellows who showed up after the car blew up. While you waited to go with the boy in the ambulance, I tracked those guys down. They *are* somehow associated with the professor. I'm not sure what that's all about either. I strongly doubt that they had anything to do with holding you and Robby.

"But these three fellows. They appear to have been totally mercenary in their efforts. I don't yet know what they were after, but they had their eyes on something that the boy's father must have had. I have no idea what their angle was."

"And none of them are going to be talking about it," Kate

retorted.

"Actually, they might be," Jack said.

"How? I doubt that the sheriff's going to let us search the cottage."

"I wasn't going to ask permission."

"We going to head back after we drop Robby off?"

"Why not? The sheriff's going to be tied up for two pay periods just catching up on paperwork. We can get Robby admitted, and then head back to the cottage. Where exactly was that? Think you can find it again?"

Chapter 85

Roger—in the nick of time

I'm sure I can. It was not far from Newberry," Kate replied. "Besides memorizing distances—they had my head pushed down. But I did check the GPS in the Rover just to confirm my calculations."

"There'll be nothing we can do for the boy once we get him admitted," Jack added. "We'll just do a U-turn and head back."

* * *

And that's exactly what they did. Once Robby was under the care of medical professionals at the hospital in Sault Ste. Marie, Jack and Kate headed right back out. They wanted to see what they could turn up at the cottage where Kate and Robby had been held.

Feeling his cell begin to vibrate, Jack checked the display and then answered it: "Roger."

"Got those murders solved yet?"

"No. And now we've got four, five more bodies to deal with."

"I hadn't heard about those yet."

"Well, with these last three … we know who killed all of them—it was the work of my daughter. Actually one managed to pass away from natural causes before she could kill him—probably a good move on his part—less trauma.

"Hey, Buddy. I'm just messing with my daughter. We're on our way back to one of the crime scenes to see what we can find. Do you have anything new for me?"

"I might. I just learned that this Tytus Gordon was negotiating with a Canadian salvage company to rent some of their equipment. Apparently they wanted to do the work, but he just wanted to rent their diving equipment and do the work himself."

"What could that be about? Any ideas?"

"Sure, lots of them. And I'm sure you're thinking the same thing," Roger replied.

"Treasure? And possibly one that was legally accessible only from the Canadian side?"

"What else? No other reason for all that secrecy."

"Then there's more to it than just Bronze Age artifacts?"

"Are you thinking gold?"

"Only two things could spark this much interest—jewels or gold. And I don't think that diamonds are involved. Has to be gold. Just makes better sense."

Both men paused for a moment, and then Roger said, "Of course, this is speculation, this treasure business. But when you look at all the people who have died regarding it, there does seem to be a basis for the speculation."

"The thing about it that throws us is the various parties involved," Jack said. "The treasure aspect would help explain motive, at least with regard to this last batch of deaths. But there seems to be more than one affiliation. That's what makes this difficult."

"What do you mean?" Roger asked.

Chapter 86

Clear as mud

Take the house, rather, the cottage, that Kate and I are headed to. That was used as a hideout, or maybe a staging area, for a group of at least three men who had hijacked an ambulance and kidnaped the son of Tytus Gordon. but it doesn't make sense to suspect that they were involved in the bombing of Mrs. Gordon's car. If they were so intent on questioning the boy, they wouldn't have tried to kill him."

"What do they say?"

"They're all dead. Remember?"

"Right—your daughter took care of that. Maybe they didn't know the boy was going to be in the car," Roger suggested.

"That's possible," Jack agreed. "The boy had been in camp. They might have planted the bomb not suspecting he'd be in the vehicle. But my guess is that they were not the bombers. I think that if they were tailing the Gordons, they were doing so in order to get their hands on them. To get information out of them. *Not* to kill them."

"Someone else then blew up the vehicle?" Roger asked.

"It would make life more simple to make these guys the bombers, but I don't think so."

"Then it was detonated with a timer. Or maybe a cell phone?" Roger suggested.

"Probably not a timer," Jack said. "Possible that it was detonated with a cell phone. But the level of sophistication just wasn't there—at least in my opinion. I'm suspecting that they set it off with an RF transmitter. Possibly by the same people who sabotaged the boat trip, and for the same reason—to silence them."

There was a significant moment of silence, finally broken by Roger.

"Run into the FBI yet?" Roger asked.

"Does that mean the marines have officially landed?"

"I don't know about that, but I'd say if they haven't yet, they're booking a flight right now."

Jack did not immediately respond, so Roger picked it back up.

"Let me see if I got this right," Roger continued. "Mrs. Gordon's dead—killed in the bombing. The son survived. Where's he at right now—you said he'd been kidnaped?"

"We got him back. And he's in the hospital—serious but stable condition. He's had it rough. We left Red with him for when he wakes up. They were at camp together and got to be pretty good friends."

"And the kidnappers—they're all dead?"

"Right. At least all that we know about for certain."

"Were they acting alone?"

"Kate and I were just discussing that," Jack replied. "They didn't strike us as being very professional. But that doesn't mean they weren't working with someone else. I'd like you to run this name: Ronald Lawrence Harper. He's from the Soo."

"Who is he? What's his significance in the case?"

"He was the leader of the three guys who kidnaped Kate and the boy. He's one of the fellows Kate killed. It'd be nice to find out who his friends are, or who he might be working with."

"I'll see what I can come up with."

"We're starting to break up … getting close to the cottage. Let me know what you find out."

"Will do," Roger replied.

"You still armed?" Jack asked.

"I am," Kate replied, producing a 9mm.

"And where did you get that?"

"The fat man gave it to me before he died. I really had not thought that he was even armed. He didn't seem to be the type to me. I'm sure glad I never acted on that assumption."

"Tell me about it. You'd better check it to be sure it's loaded."

"I already did. It's a good thing I pulled it off of him when I did because the sheriff wanted the one I used on the boss."

As they approached the turn off M-28, they spotted a large plume of black smoke rising into the sky to their left.

Chapter 87

One mystery solved—they weren't alone

D o you think?" Kate asked, ducking down to get a better look past Jack.

"Is that about the location of the cottage?" he asked.

"I think so."

"We'll know for sure in a few minutes," Jack said. "Keep your eyes open for suspicious vehicles trying to get outta there in a hurry."

By the time they reached the drive leading to the cottage, they could easily distinguish two distinct pillars of smoke, one of which was turning white. That indicated the fire department had already arrived and was pumping water on the fire.

"They must have torched the cottage and the outbuilding,"

Kate said.

"That's a lot of black smoke," Jack observed. "Something's still burning hard. That black smoke could mean a petroleum fire—perhaps the tires on that Buick."

"That's exactly what it is," Kate said. "The house, the barn, *and* the car—all torched."

They pulled down the drive and were able to drive to within fifty yards of the fire.

There was only one pumper truck on the scene, with a water supply vehicle and the fire chief's truck.

"Looks like they're letting the barn burn out," Jack said. "And those extinguishers aren't going to do much to save the car. I'll bet they've got more equipment en route. We should get out of here before we get boxed in."

Jack shoved his vehicle in reverse and sped backward toward the main road. He made it just before two additional fire vehicles entered the drive.

"There's nothing left here for us to see, *or* do," Jack said. "But this does tell us that they were not working alone. Someone did not want us or anyone else to search the cottage."

* * *

Red was sitting only a few feet from Robby's bed. He was playing games on his phone.

The doctor in charge had ordered an IV to hydrate Robby—and an antibiotic. Those were the two most critical issues to be addressed.

Infection was present but manageable.

The doctor had considered a painkiller. However, he opted to pass on it so that he could carefully monitor the boy for the first few hours.

"Red? Is that you?" Robby said, waking up for the first time since he had entered the hospital.

Red stood up and smiled at his friend.

"Where are we?" Robby asked.

Red keyed in a text and showed it to Robby.

"Hospital," Red texted.

"Where? Where's the hospital?" Robby asked.

"Soo," Red texted.

"I really hurt."

"I no."

"Where's my mom?"

Red never lied. He would not allow himself even to mislead his friend.

"Ur mom didn't make it."

Chapter 88

Meanwhile back at the hospital

W hat do you mean, 'didn't make it'?" Robby asked.
"Explosion."
"I don't remember any explosion."

Red walked over to Robby and took his hand in his and just stood there with his friend.

Both boys wept for several minutes.

It had to happen sooner or later, Red thought. *Eventually, he had to be told. I'm just glad he didn't ask about his dad. If he does, I'm going plead ignorance on that one. This kid is losing his whole life.*

After a while, Robby stopped crying and fell asleep.

Red released his friend's hand.

* * *

"Shall we head back to the hospital?" Kate asked.

"Why not. The boy seems to be the only lead we've got."

Jack felt his cell vibrating. It was Roger.

"Jack here."

"I've got a little info on your dead friend: Ronald Lawrence Harper."

"Really? That was fast."

"There's quite a dossier on him. He did some time."

"He didn't strike me as a pro."

"Oh, he's anything but a pro. He's a defrocked lawyer—disbarred eleven years ago. Did a short stint at Leavenworth as part of a plea. He knocked around after he got out. Tried to get his PI license but was refused because of his record."

"So, he contracts privately, *without* a license?"

"That's what it looks like."

"Then it was just a matter of time for him, before he went back to prison. Or got himself killed. Can you connect him to anyone specific? Kate and I are pretty sure he was not in charge of this operation. Someone torched the house where they were holding Kate and the boy—just before we could get back to it."

"He made some contacts in prison. Maybe I can find out who he's been hanging around with lately."

"That would be great. By the way, when he's not in jail, do you know where he's been living?"

"New York."

* * *

"Kate," Jack said. He had remained silent for several minutes after he ended his conversation with Roger.

Kate recognized this mood. He was thinking. And the best thing to do when her father was thinking like this was to remain silent. So that's what she did.

Finally, however, he was ready to talk.

"Okay. This is how I'm reading this. Jump in any time you want. This is what we've got. At least this is what I think we've got.

"This guy, some called him an oddball. I suppose you could call him an *explorer*. But this guy, named Tytus Gordon, wanted to cheat the system by jumping into American waters, a few hundred yards away from Big Fitz. By doing it like this, he avoided getting Canadian permission, as the Fitzgerald is in Canadian waters.

"He was going to run this mini-sub over the border—underwater, of course—and explore the Fitzgerald.

"But on the way, he claims he discovered an ancient shipwreck—one that was not on any of the charts.

"And he claims the shipwreck dates to the sixteenth century, BC.

"No one, at least none of the leading scholars, accepts his find. So, he charters the sub again and offers to take the professor, this Dr. Henry, with him to explore his supposed shipwreck.

"But Dr. Henry did not want to go with him, so the professor assigned the task to one of his subordinates.

"Now, no one knows what they found—or didn't find. Because they all ended up dead.

"And then, if that wasn't enough, this Gordon guy's wife is killed in an explosion, and his son gets kidnaped."

"I know what follows," Kate interrupted. "I enter the picture and kill all three of the boy's kidnappers. So much for witnesses, thanks to me."

"Your kills were righteous. And as far as the fat man was concerned, he died from an overdose of bacon. You didn't kill him."

"So, do you have any ideas about this guy we refer to as the boss, who he was working for? Or with?"

"None. How about you?"

"I think I heard Roger suggest that he was based out of New York? Wasn't that what he said?"

"Right. Roger said that this fellow, this Ronald Lawrence Harper, he was an attorney who got disbarred. And then he did time in a federal penitentiary—Leavenworth."

"Would be nice to find out who he hooked up with in prison."

"That's what Roger is looking into. That, and also who his friends are in New York."

"If I knew that I could have my department do some checking too."

"According to Roger," Jack continued, "this Harper guy tried to get his PI papers but couldn't because of his record."

"So he was running his operation outside the law?"

"That appears to be the case—if you can even call it an operation. What the—"

Those were the last words Jack spoke before impact.

Chapter 89

Sudden impact

He wasn't speeding. The limit along that stretch of M-28 was fifty-five. Jack had the cruise set at fifty-seven.

He couldn't avoid the collision. The empty double-trailered log hauler was headed west—Jack and Kate were going east toward the hospital.

The huge vehicle cut directly in front of them, forcing Jack to veer sharply to the left to escape hitting the truck head on.

Even though Jack did miss the front bumper as the truck shot across the highway in front of him, he wasn't so fortunate when it came to the rest of it.

The driver of the truck had intentionally jackknifed his rig, by cranking the steering wheel radically left and locking the front air brakes. This maneuver caused the twin trailers to swing toward the cab—almost perpendicular to the road.

Jack did not want to hit the drainage ditch full speed. So, once past the cab, he steered his vehicle sharply back to the right. His right front tire was still on the paved surface, and so it dug in until the weight of his vehicle shifted from it.

When both front and rear left wheels had hit the soft shoulder, his vehicle began skidding. He hit his brakes for the first time at that precise moment.

While he was able to keep all four wheels on the ground for a short fraction of a second, he knew he was not going to miss the second trailer.

The whipping action of the jackknifing truck swung the second trailer hard into the right front quarter panel of Jack's SUV, picking it entirely up off the pavement and hurling it like a hard-hit foul ball off Prince Fielder's bat.

It was a nasty impact. But because it was not straight on, Jack's momentum was redirected rather than abruptly terminated.

There was no way to tell how many times his vehicle merry-go-rounded before it landed right side up in the marsh.

Both Jack and Kate survived, largely because of their seatbelts and the structural integrity of the Tahoe.

But the crash did not leave them unscathed. In fact, neither of them had any idea how long they were unconscious.

Kate woke up first.

Chapter 90

Surveying the scene

"Dad, you okay?"

The sound of her voice brought Jack out.

"My head's splitting. But I think I'm okay," he said, pushing a deflated airbag away from his face. "How about you?"

"I'm not exactly *fine*—but I'll make it. What happened, anyway?"

"Take a look over there," Jack said, pointing to the tail end of the second trailer. That is all that remained visible from their vantage point.

"We hit the back end of that truck."

"How'd that happen? I must not have been watching."

"It was intentional," Jack said. "He tried to kill us."

"Let's go check him out," Kate said, trying to open her door but without success.

"It's stuck," she said. "Can you get yours open?"

"Mine's already open. In fact, it's altogether gone," Jack said. "Unhook and slide out over here."

Jack then jumped out and turned to help Kate.

But she had already slid out of the broken passenger-side window and was headed toward the crashed truck.

The truck had so completely jack-knifed that the front of the cab was resting against the side of the first trailer.

"I don't see a driver in there, Do you?"

"He might have been thrown out at impact," Jack offered.

"Let's take a closer look," Kate said, climbing up to get a look inside.

"What do you make of *that*?" she asked, finding the truck cab empty. "He's not there. The driver, he's gone."

"Ever see a setup like that?" Jack asked, pointing at the back of the driver's seat cockpit.

"Nascar, maybe."

"Exactly," Jack replied. "That's a Hans neck bracing system, installed with a six-point harness. "

"I'm no expert on racing," Kate said, "but from what I understand it was the crash that killed Dale Earnhardt Sr. that mandated the Hans device be installed to protect all Nascar drivers."

"And stunt drivers. Hollywood uses them in crash scenes. They're not cheap. We're looking at a couple grand right there, easy, plus installation."

"And they just left it there."

"They're pretty much custom fitted in an application like this,"

Jack said, as they both began to scrutinize the rest of the truck.

"Check that out," Kate said. "The fuel tank is virtually ripped in two, yet there's no diesel fuel spilled."

"Right. Whoever pulled this off had it calculated down to the last drop. They put in only the amount of fuel needed to reach the point they intended to kill us. That way there'd be no fire. And they must have used a chase car—someone following the truck to pick up the driver."

"Or, more likely, following us at a distance."

"Okay," Kate summarized. "The whole dynamic has changed. This now looks like a *well-organized* plot, involving some very smart people and a lot of money. At least this aspect of it looks well organized."

"What the hell is going on here?" shouted a man from the side of the road.

Chapter 91

Make-believe nurse

Jack and Kate both looked up to see Sheriff Green standing beside his car with his hands on his hips.

"I can't leave you two alone for even a minute," the sheriff quipped, "and you go ahead and break something big. So, tell me, what happened here?"

* * *

"Robby Gordon?" the nurse asked, gently waking the boy up.

"Yes."

"I'm here to administer your antibiotic," she said, removing a prefilled needle from a neatly folded cloth.

"This will poke a little, but I'll be very gentle."

Red sat up abruptly in a chair next to his friend. The nurse had not initially seen him.

"And who might you be?" she said, somewhat surprised.

"He doesn't talk," Robby said. "That's Red. He's my friend."

"So you're a friend of the Gordon kid?"

Red nodded in agreement. But then he noticed something strange happening. Robby had barely completed his sentence, and he fell asleep.

A male nurse had entered the room right behind the nurse with the needle. When he spotted Red, he turned his back so Red couldn't observe what he was doing. He took a bottle of chloroform out of his scrub and poured a liberal amount onto a hand towel. And then, stepping around the end of the bed, he quickly slapped the damp towel over Red's face.

After he was certain Red was out, the male nurse walked out of the room and retrieved a gurney he had parked just outside the door.

Within twenty seconds, the nurses had loaded the limp bodies of the two boys, covered them with blankets and headed toward the elevator. They had placed Robby on top of the gurney and Red on the bottom, where he could not be seen.

"Excuse me," the nurse in charge barked as they pushed the boys toward the elevator. "Who have you got, and where are you headed?"

The female nurse who was directing the gurney lifted the release form in the air for her to see.

"Robert Gordon," she said. "His doctor is having him transferred to Detroit Medical Center— Pediatric Burn Center."

"Let me see that," the head nurse demanded, impatiently

motioning for it to be handed to her.

After examining the paperwork, she blurted: "It looks in order. Why didn't I know about it?"

The nurse pushing the gurney smiled at her and shrugged her shoulders.

"Take this and Mr. Gordon down to discharge. I'm sure they don't know anything about it either. I'll get the authorization to release the patient, and they should have it all set for you when you get there."

"Thank you," the nurse said, taking the form back from the head nurse.

As they pushed the gurney away, the head nurse turned to an assistant. Glaring over the top of her black-rimmed glasses, she asked: "Have you ever seen either one of them before?"

"No, I haven't."

"HR keeps bringing in cheaper labor. I imagine my head will soon be on the block too. Probably already is. How about you? Are you after my job?"

The two nurses smiled at each other, as the head nurse paged the intern who had been treating the boy.

When the elevator arrived on their floor, they rolled the gurney in ahead of two people who were waiting. "Excuse us," the male nurse said. "Could you catch the next elevator? This is a bit of an emergency."

But instead of going down to discharge, they took the elevator up one level, where they had earlier parked a laundry cart. While one of them held the elevator door open, the other pulled the cart into the car and then rapidly deposited the two boys into the cart.

Once they had tossed the blankets on top of the two boys, they rolled the gurney out into the hall and pressed the button for the basement.

On the way down they removed their scrubs and replaced them with maintenance uniforms, which they had stored in the laundry cart. They then pushed the two boys out a service entrance and into a waiting laundry van.

Two blocks from the hospital, they drove the van onto a ramp and through the open roll-up door of a short semi-truck.

The kidnapping was complete.

* * *

Kate texted, "Hows Robby?"

But no one responded.

Chapter 92

Jack needs new wheels

She waited a few minutes and repeated the text—still no one texted back.

"That's strange," she said to Jack. "Red's not answering."

"Try texting to your phone. Red should still have it."

"That's what I did."

Kate and Jack had ridden back to the Soo with the sheriff and were now sitting in his office.

"Sheriff," Jack said. "Have you got a vehicle Kate and I could use? Red's at the hospital with the Gordon boy, and he's not responding to our texts. I've got an uneasy feeling."

"No, but I can arrange for a rental. Let me have a copy your driver's license. I'll have my secretary take care of it for you.

"In the meantime, I'll drive you over to the hospital. I want to check up on the boy anyway."

Jack handed him his driver's license.

* * *

"Who's texting the kids? Is that Handler?"

"Yeah, it's Handler's daughter—Kate."

"I thought your guy was supposed to take him and his daughter out today? What went wrong?"

"*Nothing* went wrong. Jeff blocked the whole road off with that log hauler. It was perfect. Handler just got lucky. He avoided a head-on collision, but he still did catch the back of the rig. Or it caught him.

"I saw the whole thing. Handler's vehicle flew like a Frisbee right into the woods. I didn't think anyone could have survived it."

"Well, they most definitely did survive. Why didn't you stick around and finish them off?"

"I got Jeff out of the truck. He was fine. But before I could confirm that the Handlers were dead, my spotter called me and said I had a county car approaching. So I took off."

"Right now the most important thing we can do is get that Gordon kid to tell us what he knows."

"According to Harper, the kid didn't know anything."

"I know what Harper said. But the kid must know something. He was very close to that worthless dad of his. Besides, he's the only one left who could possibly know where his dad hid it. We've just got to get him to talk to us."

"He's in bad shape, with his burns and all. I don't know much about it, but you can die from burns like that."

"That's why we grabbed his IV, and we know what antibiotic they'd been giving him. We can take care of him just as well as any hospital."

"You're nuts. You know that? You're absolutely nuts. There's more to treating serious burns than an IV and antibiotics."

"Look, all we have to do is keep him alive long enough to get what we need outta him. And then we let him die.

"He'll talk. But if he actually doesn't know anything about where his father might have hidden it, then we don't need him anyway. And we certainly don't need that redhead. He isn't gonna tell us anything—he can't talk."

"I think that kid is somehow related to Jack Handler. You know anything about that?"

"Yeah. Of course. The kid's his nephew."

"The redhead is Handler's nephew? For real?"

"For real. The guy who looked after the boy on Sugar Island was actually the boy's biological father. Well, he was also Handler's brother-in-law. He got himself killed last year. And then Kate became the boy's legal guardian."

"You know what you've done? You've kicked the hornets' nest. Handler is not going to back off. Not ever. The only way to get him off our backs is to kill him, *and* his daughter."

"Yeah. So? That's how we get him."

"What're you suggesting?"

"We use the kid, the redhead, to lure the Handlers in. And we set a trap for them. That's what I had in mind as soon as I realized that they were not killed in the accident."

* * *

"Jack? Roger here."

Chapter 93

No time for Roger

Jack and Kate had verified with the hospital that Robby Gordon had been discharged a little earlier and that they had no knowledge of Red's whereabouts.

The sheriff had made arrangements for a rental car for Jack, and he had dropped him off at a rental facility near Easterday and Ashmun.

Jack and Kate were just about to pull out onto Easterday when Roger called.

"Roger," Jack responded, "there's a new major wrinkle."

"What's that?"

"There was a well-orchestrated attempt to kill Kate and me. Obviously, it failed. But it involved a specially setup log hauler, stolen, of course. The driver had been dispatched with a minimal amount of fuel. He tried for a head-on but had to settle for a side-swipe."

"You guys okay?"

"Banged up a little, but not seriously injured."

"Glad to hear you made it."

"The bad news is they took Red and the Gordon kid—again. Right from the hospital. They had the proper forms, uniforms, IDs, and a laundry truck—everything they could have needed to get the boys out of the hospital. I'm revising my assessment. While I still view the first three members of this group as disappointing, a bit clumsy even, those heading it up are highly professional."

"Have you figured out how to get the kids back?"

"Not yet. We just found out they were missing."

"I can see why they'd take the Gordon boy. But why your nephew?"

"But most likely they took him because he was with Robby. Simple case of wrong place, wrong time."

Just then Jack's cell signaled an incoming text.

"Got something here. I'll call you back later," he said to Roger as he disconnected, never learning the reason Roger had called in the first place.

He looked at the text and then flashed his eyes up to meet Kate's: "It's from your cell!"

Chapter 94

Jack determines the text is bogus

U ncle Jack. You and Kate ok?"
Jack texted back: "We're good. Where are U?"
Jack slid over so Kate could see the messages and said,
"Take a look at this."

"I'm at Applebee's. Can you pick me up?"

"Kate and I'll be right there."

"Thanks."

"What do you make of this?" Jack asked his daughter.

"It's a trap of some sort. That wasn't Red. Not his texting style. And he called you 'Uncle' Jack. Not 'Unk' Jack."

"Exactly. And we don't have much time. If we don't show up in the next twenty minutes, they'll pull back."

"Why do you suppose they picked Applebee's?" Kate asked.

"Bring it up on your iPad, and let's take a look."

"Check that out," Kate said. "The I-75 northbound on-ramp is accessible from their parking lot. We pull in, they kill us, and off they go on the highway."

"That's it," Jack agreed. "We don't have any time. Let's roll."

Chapter 95

Art of setting traps

"Sheriff," Jack said, calling Sheriff Green as he headed toward the West Easterday Ave. ramp onto southbound I-75.

"Got a text from Red. He'll be at Applebee's in exactly seventeen minutes."

"You sure it's your nephew?"

"It was a text. Red has to text. And he called me Uncle Jack. I need you to help me out. I would like you to send two marked cars, lights but no sirens, west on the I-75 Business Spur and turn into Applebee's. And then just wait there."

"I can do that. Should I send the officers inside?"

"Not right away. Just wait in the lot for five minutes, lights but no sirens. If Red doesn't come out, then go in and check it out. He should be watching for you. The critical thing is the timing—no sooner than seventeen minutes, or later than nineteen."

"Okay. You gonna meet us there?"

"No. Can't. But I'll explain later. Gotta go."

Kate thought a minute and then said, "So we head south on I-75 past the 3 Mile Road overpass, cross the median, and wait on the overpass until we see a car cut through the grass and onto the ramp."

"Almost—except the highway passes *under* 3 Mile Road. So, we cross the median south of 3 Mile Road. We head north past the 3 Mile Road underpass, and park in the median just before the on-ramp dumps onto I-75 but far enough north to have a good view of the whole on-ramp. We have to be able to spot the car jumping the curb at Applebee's."

"And then we follow them to where they're holding Red and Robby," Kate finished Jack's plan. "We've got sixteen minutes. You're gonna have to step on it."

Neither Jack nor Kate spoke another word until they neared 3 Mile Road. As they approached the on-ramp going the opposite direction, Jack slowed the car to size up where he would need to stop to get a good view of where he suspected the kidnappers to cut across.

"Right there," he said. "We can get a good look from there. We'll just have to time it perfectly."

"What if the sheriff's late, or early?"

"We're going to have to assume he won't be. What's our time look like?"

"Nine minutes, twenty seconds. We have just over seven minutes. Is that too long?"

"Perfect," Jack replied.

"Okay. We're going under 3 Mile Road right now. In one minute and twenty seconds, we should look for an emergency vehicle crossover. If we don't find one, then we'll have to just hit the median and hope for the best.

"There!" Kate exclaimed, pointing ahead. "That's our crossover."

"It is, but it's too early. I'm going to pull off on the shoulder and give it forty seconds."

Just as Jack hit his four-ways and slowed, a state police cruiser pulled in behind him.

"This is not good," Jack moaned, reaching for the proof of insurance and registration.

"Let me have the insurance papers," Kate said, snatching them just before he did.

"May I see your license, registration, and proof of insurance," the officer requested.

"I can't seem to find the paperwork. It's a rental. But here's my driver's license," Jack said, handing the state trooper a fake driver's license he always had with him for such occasions.

"I'll run your license and the plate. You keep looking for the registration—it should be with the vehicle."

As soon as the officer had seated himself behind the wheel of his patrol car, Kate handed Jack half a dozen meaningless sheets of paper that were lying on the seat. And Jack handed Kate a long sharp-bladed knife.

Jack then jumped out of the car waving the papers for the officer to see.

Just before Jack reached the rear of his car, he allowed the air that was stirred up by a passing semi to snatch the papers from his grasp and onto the highway.

Using that as a distraction, Kate jumped out of her side and darted undetected to the right front passenger side tire of the patrol car and drove the knife through its sidewall.

She then sneaked back in the car.

Meanwhile, Jack feigned going after the papers, prompting the trooper to get out of his patrol car and command Jack to get back in his car, which Jack did.

Immediately upon shutting his door, Jack shoved the shifter into drive and shot across the emergency crossover.

The state trooper tried to pursue but was unable because of the flat tire.

"We're exactly twelve seconds behind schedule," Kate said.

"We'll be fine," Jack said, killing the lights. "There's not another northbound car in sight. The first car that hits the highway from that on-ramp will be our suspects."

Jack did not have to wait long.

"Would you look at that!" he shouted in amazement.

Chapter 96

So far so good

Exactly as planned, Jack had pulled off southbound I-75 and onto the median, parking at the precise spot he had picked out.

And just as expected, no sooner than had he come to a complete stop, both Jack and Kate spotted the suspect car at the same time.

"That's them! I saw the headlights jump on that car that's headed this way on the ramp. They bounced the curb just like we thought they would."

Jack was pleased that their plan had worked so far. But he was concerned about tailing the car without giving himself away.

Jack waited longer than he would have liked before proceeding to allow a large semi-truck to pass.

As they pulled out, Kate took another look back at Applebee's.

"Holy cow! There must be half a dozen cop cars in the parking lot. No wonder these guys were in such a hurry to get out of there."

Jack waited until he had pulled in behind the truck before he turned his lights on.

"What if they head into Canada?" Kate posed.

There was one more exit before the entrance to the bridge to Canada.

"They've got a car full of firearms," Jack said. "Not likely they'd be taking them across the border. Unless … unless they ditched them right after they pulled onto the ramp, before they reached us."

"All academic. I'm sure that state trooper has a call out on us," Kate said. "We wouldn't have a chance at the border."

"I doubt they're going that far. And I'm positive we aren't."

Kate double-checked to be certain the 9mm she was carrying had a round in the chamber and a full clip.

Jack pulled to within striking distance should their target have appeared to be passing the last exit. If the car was headed to Canada, Jack would have rammed them.

"This is challenging," Kate said. "Can't let them know we're following. And don't want to kill them. Not yet."

"They're braking, and signaling," Jack said. They're thinking we might be cops. They are being very deliberate."

Chapter 97

Jack's plan hits snag

W hen we get to the stop sign at Easterday," Kate said, "they're going to know this is not a cop car."

"If they turn east, toward town, we'll follow. But if they head west, we'll have to see … not so much going on over there. We can't afford to have them make us."

"They're turning west," Kate said, observing their turn signal.

"Duck down," Jack told her as they pulled in behind the car. "Best if they think there's only one person in this car. I'll yell if they come back at us. Shoot for feet or face, because they're likely to be wearing armor.

"I'm seeing only a driver," Jack said. "They're doing the same thing. I suspect a driver plus at least one passenger."

"Do you think they made us?"

"No. They're just being careful. Okay, stay down, we're passing over I-75."

"Are you familiar with what's west of the highway?"

"Not unless they turn north on Portage. We're up the creek if they don't. For sure they'll know we're tailing them. Let's hope for Portage."

"Stop sign?" Kate asked, still ducking down, pistol in hand.

The car containing the suspected gunmen had turned left on West Easterday at the end of the ramp and then had passed over the highway. A right at West Easterday would have led into downtown Sault Ste. Marie.

Immediately on the other side of the overpass was a three-way stop signal.

A left turn at that signal would take you south on I-75, straight ahead led into a less frequently traveled industrial section of Sault Ste. Marie, and a right at the signal led onto West Portage Avenue. This street twisted and turned its way along the Whitefish Bay shoreline—under the International Bridge to Canada—and eventually straightened out and paralleled the Soo Locks.

"Yeah. And they're moving to the right turn lane."

"On Portage?"

"They are. I detected some hesitation on their commitment. Almost like they were waiting for me to make the first move. But it's definitely right on Portage."

"They're turning into the welcome center."

"Really?" Kate said. "That's a circular drive. No way out, except back onto Portage."

"They've either figured us out or are about to. Yup, there they are very discreet. They circled around and now they're behind us."

"They're not going to lead us to Red now, at least not right away," Kate surmised.

Jack agreed. He was no longer the pursuer. He knew that at some point, probably quite soon, he and Kate would come under attack. So he hatched a plan.

Chapter 98

Revision or improvision?

I'm going to time the next traffic light for red. That'll be up here at Ashmun. Prepare to get rear-ended—*violently* rear-ended!"

"That's a long way," Kate said. "Over a mile. Think they'll pull something before that?"

"Stay down and ready. I'm not so sure they're totally convinced it's us."

Jack spotted his opportunity. He was approaching Ashmun St., and the light was green. He decelerated but did not brake. The light turned red.

The car following them had dropped back about two hundred yards. But that distance was now closing quickly as Jack and Kate slowed.

"The passenger is not visible. But I'll bet he doesn't have his seat belt on. In fact, I'll bet neither one of them are buckled," Jack said, as he reached back to adjust his headrest.

Jack's 2013 black Chevy Impala was now stopped at Ashmun St. Jack waited until the tailing car closed to within seventy-five feet of the rear of his car.

Jack then revved the engine to two thousand RPMs.

"Prepare for impact," he said as he slid the shifter into reverse.

The distance between the two vehicles closed quickly.

The front-wheel drive Impala is an amazingly gutsy vehicle off the line, particularly when in reverse. Rapid acceleration backward shifts the weight of the vehicle to the front wheels, driving it downward creating greater traction. The three-hundred-horsepower 3.6-liter V6 engine barely spun at all—even on start up.

There was nothing the driver of the rear car could do to avoid the crash. Initially, he didn't realize what was happening. By the time he did, Jack's rented Impala was speeding at him at over twenty-five miles per hour. Add that to the rear car's forward speed, and the fact that Jack had been correct in his belief that neither of the men in the car was wearing a seatbelt, when the impact occurred both men were launched forward in a horrendous fashion.

The driver's airbag exploded in his chest and face, knocking the air from his lungs and rendering him temporarily helpless.

The passenger was not so lucky—his airbag had been disabled. The force of his forward momentum shot him through the windshield and onto the trunk of Jack's Impala. There he lay, unconscious and bleeding out. Jack determined later that it was the windshield wiper that ripped open his left carotid artery.

Kate had prepared herself for the impact by curling up against the back of the passenger seat. She was not stunned even though on impact the front of the Impala lifted nearly a foot off the pavement.

By the time the front of the Impala had landed, she had flipped her body around to get out. Finding her door jammed, she rolled the window down and scrambled through it.

Blood from the passenger was squirting upward and onto the rear window of the Impala. She knew immediately that he was dying.

By resting his head on the headrest before the crash and relaxing his body, Jack also emerged from the car uninjured. Fortunately for him, his door had not jammed.

He arrived at the driver's door before the airbag had deflated.

Jack smashed the side glass out with his pistol and grabbed the driver by his jacket. With a single powerful sustained pull, he yanked the man up off his seat and through the opening.

The man landed helplessly on the pavement. Jack patted the unconscious driver down, removing a Glock from a holster under his jacket and a small J-frame from a holster on his right calf. Jack then cuffed the man's hands behind his back with a heavy-duty tie-wrap and dragged him up onto the sidewalk.

"How's your guy?" he yelled over to Kate.

Chapter 99

Surprise—surprise

"My guy's very dead. And yours?" Kate replied.

"Very lucky. If we didn't need him to tell us where Red and Robby are, he wouldn't stay lucky."

Jack then unceremoniously rolled the man onto his back, and shoved his knee deep into his chest.

"That armor isn't helping now, is it?" he said, as the man grimaced in pain.

The force of the airbag had broken three ribs, so Jack's knee exacerbated the pain exponentially.

"Where you keeping the boys?" Jack asked, lifting his knee from the man's midsection to allow him to talk.

Not hearing any response, Jack dropped his knee again into the man's midsection again. He could feel the broken ribs as he continued to apply pressure.

The pain was so intense the man could not cry out.

"You'd better start talking to me, or you're not gonna live to read this accident report. I'm gonna ask you again," Jack said, taking his weight off of the man. "Where are the boys?"

"Stop! Please just stop," the driver moaned. "I'll tell you. But don't hurt me anymore. Please don't hurt me anymore."

Jack didn't hurt the man again. But not because he started talking. Jack looked up and saw a pair of very large headlights heading his way at a high rate of speed.

"Oh my god!" he shouted. "Kate, run!"

She did, and Jack ran as well. At the very moment Jack and Kate reached safety, the crash occurred.

Chapter 100

Crash-bang-boom

B y the time the noise had subsided, Jack's rented Impala was upside down well beyond the traffic signal at the Portage Street—Ashmun Street intersection. It might have slid a full block beyond the light had it not sideswiped several parked cars.

The car that had been following Jack was still rolling slowly eastward. The dead passenger had been re-deposited into it through the broken front windshield.

About seventy feet to the east was the back end of a semi-trailer. Jack looked over at Kate on the opposite side of the street: "You're okay. Right?"

"Yeah. And you?"

"I'm fine."

"How about the driver?"

"I've got him over here. He's feeling a bit poor, but I think it could be worse."

"Shall we check it out?" Kate asked.

Jack did not have a chance to respond. He was cut short by the most god-awful noise he had ever heard.

Chapter 101

Red to the rescue

Jack's eyes fixed on the cab of the truck, which after the crash had rolled into a group of parked cars and had finally come to a complete stop. The engine was still running, but the shifter had jarred into neutral on impact.

Just then Red jumped to the street and let out another blood-curdling scream.

"Red!" Jack shouted. "It's Red! I can't believe this."

Both Kate and Jack raced to him.

Shouting and signaling as best he could, Red pounded on the side of the trailer and pointed.

It was then that they observed that Red's hands were tied

together.

"Robby in there?" Jack asked.

Red nodded his head violently and used his index finger to form a gun.

"And there's someone in there who has a gun? Is that right?"

Red frantically nodded his head to confirm Kate's words.

"Go over to the sidewalk, and duck behind a parked car. Now!" Jack commanded.

As soon as Red was safe, Jack unlatched the doors on the trailer and swung one of them wide open.

Parked inside the trailer was a medical transport vehicle, and pinned underneath the rear of it was a large woman.

Jack correctly determined that the woman had become lodged under the vehicle when Red crashed into the two stopped cars.

Jack and Kate both jumped into the trailer. Kate popped open the doors of the transport vehicle while Jack pulled the woman out from under it.

"This is my last tie-wrap, so you'd better be the only clown back here," he said for Kate's benefit.

Lying on the floor of the transport vehicle was a half-open brown paper bag. Sticking out of it was a large nurse's uniform.

Once he had secured the woman's hands, Jack then joined Kate in the transport vehicle to check on the boy.

Chapter 102

Story not over

R obby, my man," Jack said. "You look pretty darn good to me."

The boy smiled but said nothing.

Kate had taken his hand in hers. Her eyes sparkled.

Red had waited on the sidewalk for as long has he could. Now standing at the open rear of the trailer, he placed his two hands on the bed and lunged forward, somehow lifting his feet off the pavement using his elbows. Kicking his right leg up, he spun his body around and pulled his left leg up and then rolled in, all in a single smooth motion.

"Hey, kiddo," Jack said to him. "Looks like your friend is just fine. Come on up here and check for yourself. And maybe I'll untie your hands for you."

Red slid in next to Robby. He was more interested in checking out the status of his friend than in having his uncle Jack remove the white nylon rope that secured his hands. The boys' extended greeting was silently communicative.

Just then the engine of the big rig was shut off.

"I'd say we have company," Kate said, pointing her 9mm toward the rear doors of the trailer and assuming a defensive position on one knee.

Jack pulled Red behind him and did the same, pointing his firearm in the same direction.

"Thud, thud, thud."

Chapter 103

As might be expected

The clamorous banging reverberated throughout the trailer—three events, no more. Both Jack and Kate were apprehensive about their "fish in a barrel" predicament.

"Jack Handler, and I would guess Kate. Is that you in there?"

Kate and Jack lowered their firearms and exchanged a glance of relief. It was Sheriff Green.

"I'm guessing the both of you are all set to shoot another sheriff. Well, unless the guns you are holding are licensed by the State of Michigan, and both of you have on your person valid permits, then I suggest you get rid of them ASAP. Because I'm about to come on board, and I wouldn't want to arrest you, at least not until you've told me your side of the story."

"Sheriff," Jack shouted. "Get yourself up here and see what we've found."

The sheriff first pointed the blinding beam of his five-cell Maglite in Jack's face and then in Kate's.

"Turn that thing off before you do some permanent damage. Please," Jack requested impatiently.

The emergency backup power built into the transport vehicle provided minimal but adequate LED lighting. The bright beam of Sheriff Green's old-school flashlight was physically painful to the dilated eyes of Jack and Kate.

"I would assume those are our two missing boys," the sheriff said, switching off his light and lifting himself up into the trailer.

"They actually look pretty good. At least better than I feared. How come you're keeping your nephew tied up? Maybe I'll have to have a talk with CPS about this."

"Sheriff. We've got to get Robby to the hospital," Kate admonished.

"Yes we do," Sheriff Green agreed. "And this time I'm assigning a deputy to protect him—24/7."

Sheriff Green radioed in for an ambulance and tow trucks. And then he asked, "Who gets the bill for all this damage? Who was driving this rig?"

Kate looked back at Red, who was still tucked in behind Jack. And she smiled.

"You're kidding me!" the sheriff said. "The kid was driving the semi?"

Sheriff Green smiled as he quipped: "Well, I can sure see why you've got his hands tied. This redhead of yours is dangerous."

"He sure is. And I'm sure that this gal here will agree, *if* she wakes up," Jack agreed, pointing at the motionless woman still lying near the rear of the transport vehicle.

"Oh, and by the way," Jack said to the sheriff. "We've got one more fellow cuffed. He's on the sidewalk. And one dead. I'm not exactly sure where his body ended up after Red parked this big rig."

"I found him. He's lying on the front seat of that car with all the firearms in it. It looks like an arms vault—assault rifles, anti-personnel shotguns, you name it."

"Those are the fellows your cars chased out of Applebee's earlier tonight. They were trying to lure Kate and me out to their party."

The sheriff thought for a moment and then said, "You know, Handler, I had the most interesting call tonight, from a state trooper."

Chapter 104

Trouble trouble trouble

Apparently an older man and a young, attractive woman shoved a knife through one of his tires while he was running their plates. The descriptions he gave sounded a lot like you two. And they were driving a 2013 Impala. Know anything about that?"

"Must have been traumatic for him," Kate chuckled "Poor fellow. Sounds like he might have run into a modern-day Bonnie and Clyde. Lucky she didn't steal his trousers."

"I don't see any humor in it," the sheriff replied. "And Handler, you're pushing it. I didn't like the way you worked to begin with. And I certainly don't like running interference for your escapades, especially when it involves other agencies."

"I appreciate what you're saying, Sheriff. But keep in mind our conversation earlier, at the bomb scene. You agreed with me that we were going to work together on this. You're in this as deeply as I am. It's too late to back out now. I'm virtually your partner, Kate too. And Red. Hell, Red just saved your kidnap victim and single-handedly broke up this little gang. If it weren't for him, you'd not be able to report this amazing success."

"That's what's pissing me off," the sheriff said. "You're right about all that. But you're so damn messy. Everybody dies around you."

"Now that's not true. Mostly the bad guys die. You know that. Just look around—two criminals are cuffed, a third one is dead. And, on this day, all the good guys get to live a little longer. We may be messy, Sheriff, but you'll have to admit that we're effective."

"Tonight, Handler. You and Kate are going to come down to my office and give me a full statement. And bring your nephew with you. I'll need to hear from him as well."

"Sheriff," a deputy called out. "You need to see this."

Chapter 105

The sheriff wants a meeting

Tonight, Handler. In my office—*tonight,* before the sun comes up!"

Sheriff Green walked to the open end of the trailer and said, "Yes, Deputy, what's up?"

"Come over here and check out the prisoner—the fellow Handler cuffed and left on the sidewalk."

"Okay. But what's the big deal?"

"I'll have to show you. And you might want to bring Handler over here too."

"Jack. Can you join us for a minute?"

"Keep your eye on these kids," Jack said to Kate with a smile.

"Red especially. Don't want him stealing another car ... *or* a truck. I'll be back as soon as I can. Looks like all three of us have to sit down with the sheriff tonight."

"I'll keep tabs on them," Kate replied as she untied Red's hands. "Actually, I wouldn't mind hearing what Red has to text about his adventures tonight. I'll bet that's going to be interesting."

Jack jumped off the trailer and caught up with the sheriff and his deputy.

"Isn't my prisoner doing so well?" Jack asked. "He was just fine when I left him."

"Well," the deputy said, "he ain't doin' so well anymore."

"I don't know what he could be bitchin' about. I made sure to put the tie-wrap on loose enough for circulation. Not because I wanted to be nice to him, but I'm sure he's got a lot of info that I'd like to hear about."

"Then you're saying that you had nothing to do with the screwdriver that's sticking in his back. Is that right, Mr. Handler?"

Jack could not believe what he saw. There he was, the driver whose life he had saved only moments earlier, lying on his stomach right where Jack had dragged him. And, just as the deputy had said, a large screwdriver was driven into his back and through his heart so that only the handle protruded from his large print Hawaiian shirt.

"Twelve minutes ago this guy was alive and complaining. I was about to question him when I heard that semi bearing down on us. Had I wanted him dead, I could have left him on the street. Jack quickly rifled through the dead man's pockets but found no ID."

"Take a look around. It's after midnight," the sheriff said. "There's no one on the street, except us. Do you recall seeing anyone out here when the crash happened? *Anyone?*"

"No," Jack replied. "But there must have been someone we missed. Kate and I both ran to the truck immediately after impact. That has to be when it happened."

Jack, who had been kneeling over the body, stood to his feet and looked back toward the truck. He noticed something.

"Sheriff, did you, or one of your men, open the door on that sleeper?" he asked.

"*I* didn't," Sheriff Green replied. "But I did notice that it was open when I got here. I looked in but didn't see anything. I assumed you must have opened it. Or that it flew open on impact."

Chapter 106

The man was a doctor

I didn't," Jack said. "There must have been someone in there that whole time, even while Red was escaping. Let's check with him."

The three men hurriedly headed back to the trailer.

"Red, did you know that you had a passenger in that sleeper?" Jack asked.

Red shook his head, his eyes wide with astonishment.

"Was there a second man, or woman? Besides this one?" Jack asked, pointing to the still body of the woman half-pinned in the back of the truck.

Red nodded.

"But you had no idea he was in the sleeper?"

Red slowly shook his head. And then he motioned for a cell phone.

"He needs a cell phone, Sheriff. He wants to send a text," Kate said.

Sheriff Green tossed Red his cell phone.

"I thnk he was a doc. He hlpd Rbby."

Kate was watching over Red's shoulder as he texted and was reading out loud what he was entering.

"That makes total sense," she said. "Robby is doing *exceptionally* well. Someone with training has been administering his meds. He doesn't even have a fever anymore."

"If he was in the sleeper, why didn't he jump you from behind?" Jack asked.

Red's head popped up. Almost instantly he bolted to the rear of the trailer, motioning the whole way for Jack to follow.

The deputy remained with Robby while Jack, Kate, and the sheriff followed Red to the cab of the truck. There he showed them the two-by-four that had been used to secure the door separating the cab from the sleeper.

"Did they sometimes keep you in the sleeper?" Jack asked.

Red nodded enthusiastically.

"That makeshift lock saved your life. The doctor was trapped in the sleeper until after the crash. Then, when we all ran into the back of the trailer, he must have exited the side door, found his buddy, and pushed that screwdriver through his heart."

"Talk about luck," the sheriff said. "That two-by-four was definitely all that saved these kids. Just amazing."

"Do you think you could take us back to where they were holding you?" Jack asked.

Red nodded.

"How about it, sheriff? Shall we check it out?"

Chapter 107

Red explains

"Ask him if there are anymore back there," the sheriff said.
Red held up four fingers.

"There are four more?" Jack asked.

Red shook his head.

"A total of four?"

Red nodded. And then he thought for a moment. Rocking his hand, palm down, back and forth for Jack to see, he locked his jaw and bared his teeth. That signaled to Jack that Red was not sure about something. He then held up five fingers.

"Four, *maybe* five?" Jack interpreted.

Red nodded.

"That means only the doctor is missing for sure. And perhaps one more," Jack offered. "We've got two dead here. That's the two who were in the car. Surviving we've got the doctor. And the one we suspect picked up the doctor. And this female."

"She's dead as well," Kate said.

"She is?"

"Yeah," Kate said. "While you went with the sheriff, I took her pulse. I think she might have snapped her neck on impact."

"So, we've one survivor for sure—the doctor," Sheriff Green said.

"Let's see if Red can take us back to where they were staying," Jack suggested.

"I'm staying with Robby," Kate quickly offered. "This poor kid has had enough excitement for his entire lifetime."

"You up to it?" the sheriff asked Red.

Red nodded his head, confirming his willingness, as he handed the cell phone back to the sheriff.

"We've got an ambulance on the way for the boy," Sheriff Green told Kate. "And a second ambulance for these two, three guys. You stick with the boy and let the coroner mop up the rest."

"Sounds good, Sheriff."

"Let's go check this out."

The three of them walked over to the sheriff's car. Jack insisted Red ride in the front passenger seat while he got in the back.

"For a minute there I thought you were going to wrestle me for the keys," the sheriff teased Red.

Chapter 108

Red retraces

Neither Red nor Jack verbally responded although both were smiling at the sheriff's humor.

"Okay, Son, anything around here look familiar?" the sheriff asked as they drove west down Portage Street.

Red nodded.

"Should I keep going on Portage Street?"

Red did not know the name of the street, so he just pointed straight ahead.

After a few more minutes, Red sat straight up and grew more attentive.

"Still look right?" Sheriff Green asked.

Red nodded again. And then, after another minute, he pounced on the dash and began slapping it.

Sheriff Green slowed down.

Red grabbed the sheriff's shoulder and pointed off to the left.

"The truck stop," Jack said. "That figures. Is that where the rig was parked, all the time?"

Red nodded.

"That's smart," Jack said. "Hiding out in the open like that. A truck with a reefer can be parked at a truck stop for a couple days, and no one gives it a second thought."

The sheriff pulled in, and he and Red got out. But Jack remained in the back of the patrol car because his cell vibrated.

"I've got a call—I catch up with you," Jack said.

Chapter 109

Roger completes his thought

Roger. Don't you ever sleep?" Jack quipped.

"Doesn't seem like it. At least not when I'm dealing with you."

"Right," Jack said. "We got interrupted earlier. You got something for me, don't you?"

"Maybe. Maybe something on this Harper guy. When he was in prison, at Leavenworth. He buddied up with a couple of guys. One was a real pro—an armored car specialist. Reputedly he had a real affinity for firepower."

"Got a name?"

"Richardson, Thomas Raymond Richardson—better known as

Tommy Ray Richardson."

Jack opened his door and shouted in the sheriff's direction: "Hey, Sheriff, did you get any info off the other fellow, the one in the car with the guns?"

Sheriff Green turned toward Jack and said, "Yeah. There was a New York license in his wallet—Thomas Richardson. Why?"

"I'll tell you later."

"Well, we've got your Richardson right here in the Soo," Jack said.

"And you don't need to tell me—he's dead, right?"

"Of course—guys like that don't give up anything while they're still breathing. So, tell me what you know about this Richardson."

"That's where it gets interesting. While Richardson did get convicted for the armored car robbery, it was rumored that he was involved in numerous precious metals heists, mostly in the New York area."

"Armed robberies?"

"Not always. However, that was his specialty. He would walk right in the front door of one of those "We Buy Gold" shops, brandishing an anti-personnel shotgun, while his partner would clean out the safe. And he wasn't shy about using the shotgun. In one case he killed four people—three customers and the clerk."

"I thought they used a floor safe?"

"His partner was a safecracker. We don't have a name on him, but we think he used a linear amplifier to jam wireless alarm signals. They were good. It took them less than three minutes from the time they walked in the door. They were pulling these off every other day for a month, up and down the east coast. And then, a week ago, they stopped."

"He wasn't running it on his own. Must have been an organization behind it. Right?"

"Russian, in fact, not just Russian Mafia. But this group answered directly to a Russian oligarch."

"They're after the gold, all of it, or as much as possible."

"Right, and anyone getting in their way dies."

"You think this business up here has anything to do with that?"

Chapter 110

Major connections

I have no solid evidence pointing to it," Roger continued. "Except for the *people* involved. That's what this Richardson does—he steals gold for the Russians."

"There's no gold to steal up here—not in the quantity that you might find in a place like New York or Hollywood, at least not that I know about.

"You said that he had two friends," Jack said. "What can you tell me about the *second* fellow?"

"He was a doctor, an MD," Roger replied.

* * *

Tap, tap, tap. Red was trying to get Jack's attention.

Jack looked up at Red, who was standing outside the sheriff's car. He signaled to Jack that Sheriff Green wanted him to join him.

"Roger," Jack interrupted, "it looks like the sheriff's requesting my presence, so I should go. That is an interesting angle—I'll see what I can turn up around here. Keep in touch."

"Where you taking me?" Jack asked as he stepped out of the car.

Red pointed toward the rear of the truck stop. Red took off trotting, and Jack followed at a substantially slower pace.

The truck stop was well known. It was easy on and off Interstate I-75, particularly for northbound traffic. Frequently truckers would pull into its huge crushed limestone parking area and transfer parts of their cargo to smaller trucks for local deliveries.

Because it was located right before the entrance to the Sault Ste. Marie International Bridge, often Canadian merchants and distributors would meet up with semis at the truck stop to fulfill orders. For an hourly fee, the facility would rent forklifts to aid in the transfer of merchandise.

It was the perfect place to park a truck for a few days.

Red had almost disappeared behind the truck stop restaurant before Jack caught up with him. It was obvious that the boy was eager to show his uncle something.

"Back here, Jack. The boy has something he wants to show you."

Chapter 111

The pictures

J ack immediately spotted the sheriff. He was standing beside a
white Chevy Tahoe. As Jack got closer, he noticed that the rear
hatch was open, as was the passenger door.

"This is quite the talented lad—this nephew of yours. Did you
teach him how to break into cars? I usually can't even get into one
of these with a Slim Jim. But I look the other way, for just a moment,
and he pops it open."

"I didn't teach him to do that. He picked that up on his own."

"Well, as best as I can tell from what Red was showing me, this
Tahoe belonged to the doctor and his friends. As you can see, it
has New York plates.

"And right over here, this is where they had parked the semi— the one the boy used to escape."

"How long had they been parked here?" Jack asked.

"The manager said they pulled in three days ago, and that they were staying day to day. He was a little suspicious that there didn't seem to be much activity—just the back and forth with the Tahoe. But he doesn't ask questions, as long as he gets paid.

"Here's the interesting part. In the back of the Tahoe. Take a look at this and tell me what you think."

Jack followed the sheriff around to the open hatch.

"What do you make of these pictures?"

Spread out on the floor in the back of the Tahoe were several eight-by-ten images—all taken underwater. They depicted what looked like copper ingots. They were strewn about the wreck of a wooden ship.

"This must be Gordon's ancient ship," Jack said. "What would these guys be doing with these images?"

"Those aren't the images that they were interested in," the sheriff said with a gleam in his eye. "But these are."

The sheriff removed three additional images from a white USPS envelope and spread them out on top of the others.

"Look at those puppies shine," Jack said. "I've never seen copper that looked like that."

Chapter 112

If it shines like gold ...

A nd they're laying right in there with the corroded copper ingots," the sheriff said, "like they were on the same ship when it went down."

"That's what's attracted all this high-powered attention. Gordon found *gold*, and apparently a lot of it. How much would you say was here?"

"We're looking at three ingots in this cluster," the sheriff said. "And who's to say that there wouldn't be more that was covered up with sand on the bottom. If you look carefully, you can see something that looks like an ingot under the surface, another one over here, and several more in this other picture. I'd say that there were probably at least ten gold ingots at this site—perhaps more. Who knows how many got covered up through the years?"

"I'd guess they'd weigh about two hundred pounds each. That's a ton of pure gold. That would amount to almost as much as you've accumulated in your IRA, wouldn't it Sheriff?"

"At least $40 million, at today's prices. And I suspect there'd be more."

"Where do you suppose it is—the gold in the pictures?"

"No doubt that's what they were trying to pry out of the boy," the sheriff said.

"I'm sure," Jack replied.

Both men stood for a moment looking at the images, and then Jack said, "Okay, it is virtually certain that the gold remains wherever this Gordon guy hid it. That is, unless these fellows found it. Wouldn't you agree?"

"If these guys had found it, they'd be long gone or at least fixin' to go."

"My next question is, where'd it come from?" Jack asked. "Those are very roughly-formed ingots. In fact, they are in exactly the same shape and size as the copper ingots. Were they mining gold back then, whenever *then* was?"

"You don't know? Not only was gold mined in the UP throughout history, we're about to have a new gold rush."

"What do you mean?"

"I guess that means you haven't heard about it. Over by Stephenson, in the western part of the UP, not far from the Wisconsin border, they've found a large deposit of gold. Even if nothing else is discovered, it will rank in the top ten deposits of gold in the world."

"No kidding," Jack said, his amazement obvious. "Then the gold that Gordon found at the bottom of Lake Superior could have been mined in the same area, right along with the copper?"

"Wouldn't have ended up in that Minoan ship if it was mined anywhere else," the sheriff replied.

Chapter 113

Jack: "This has to make sense"

That's all very interesting," Jack said. "I can now understand why these guys were so intent on finding out what this Gordon kid knew. But what still isn't so clear is why they would have *killed* the father before they wrestled the gold away from him. That part of the equation doesn't add up."

"Or the kid's mother, for that matter," the sheriff added. "Why would they kill her?"

"Exactly. If they did not have the info they needed, why would they eliminate the only people who might have been able to help them?"

"These guys, the doctor and his friends, seemed to have been pretty well organized." Jack said. "But that business with the boat, that has a different feel to it. Almost as though a different group perpetrated it. And perhaps for a different reason."

Both the sheriff and Jack were deep in thought when Red tugged on Jack's arm.

"Yeah, son, What're you thinking?" Jack asked the boy.

Red jumped into the back of the Tahoe and pushed some still moist soil from the floor into the palm of his opposite hand. And then he showed it to Jack and the sheriff.

"What does that appear to be?" Jack asked the sheriff.

The sheriff took a close look at it, and then he examined the floor of the Tahoe.

"Take a look at that," he said. "The carpet has been flattened out here, like something very heavy and flat had been setting on it."

"Like a gold ingot? Or maybe a *bunch* of them?"

"Definitely could be," Sheriff Green agreed. "Forensics could tell us for sure. But whatever was setting right there was very heavy and was about the same size as the ingots we spotted in those images."

"Red," Jack said, looking the boy in the eyes. "Do you recall seeing any of these fellows using another vehicle around here?"

Red thought about the question and then requested the sheriff's cell phone by mimicking the motions of texting.

The sheriff complied.

"1 time. I herd truk. Jeep I thnk. Man tlk to doc."

"Did you catch any of their conversation?" Jack asked.

"? 'Did U gt it all?' herd tossng stuff into Jeep thn left."

"When did this happen?" Jack asked.

"2 – 3 hrs."

"Okay," Jack said. "That puts a different spin on it. It now sounds like the boy did remember something. And then shared the information with the doctor. The doctor then actually found the gold, and he transferred it into a Jeep. Could be Red and Robby escaped in the nick of time. They didn't need them anymore. They tried to kill Kate and me. They thought we would get in their way."

"Sounds like the doctor was mopping up," the sheriff said. "When he drove the screwdriver through his buddy's heart. He probably met up with the guy in the Jeep downtown, right after the crash. Probably called him from inside the sleeper, while Red was driving it."

"Son," Jack asked, "can you tell us what that doctor looked like?"

Chapter 114

Dr. Crooked Nose

Sheriff Green handed his cell back to Red.

Red immediately began to text: "Nt like doc. No whte robe. Old. Yngr thn U. Oldr thn shrf. Tlkd funny."

Red then looked up at Jack and pushed his nose to the side.

"He had a crooked nose?" Jack asked.

Red nodded and continued texting: "Blck glsses. Ink. lot of ink. Showered. Rst not."

Red quit texting, looked up at Jack and shrugged his shoulders.

"Is that about it?"

Red nodded and started to hand the phone back to the sheriff.

But just before the sheriff could take it, Red took it back and texted one more message:

"Unk Jack. Go see Buddy?"

Jack read what he had written and smiled in agreement.

Jack showed the sheriff what Red had texted.

"What's that all about?"

"Red's dog—Buddy. He has been staying at the resort for the past week, while Red was in camp. Red thinks it's time to go home and get him.

The sheriff smiled at Red and said, "Son, if you think of anything else, let me know. Okay?"

Red smiled and broke into a run back to the sheriff's car.

Jack and the sheriff watched the boy take off, and then they headed back to the car as well.

"Red and the Gordon kid can identify the doctor," the sheriff said. "Is that a problem? That is, do you think that he and the guy in the Jeep will just want to split, now that they've got the gold? Or will they think of the boys as loose ends?"

"I think they're following orders from the Russian mafia. Their boss has ordered them back now that they have the gold. The boys are not a problem for the boss."

"Russian mafia?" Sheriff Green fired back in disbelief. "Really? What makes you think that?"

"According to one of my sources, there is a possible connection between the Russian mob and at least one of the fellows killed today, the one who was trying to shoot you. Ronald Lawrence Harper.

"And this doctor, his serious ink and broken nose sound like he's done some hard time. Possibly with this Harper. Just a hunch. But, if I'm right, their organization is going to want to get their hands on the gold first. And then, if they determine that the boys pose a problem, then they will send someone else up here to take care of it."

Sheriff Green was not happy to hear those words.

"That's all I need—more people killed. Handler, I'm so sick of your face. Every time I see you, people die ... *violently*. You're like my personal harbinger of death."

"Sheriff, I've not fired my gun in weeks."

"You don't have to shoot anyone—but people still keep dying around you. Over the past few days alone, right here in my county, seven people, at least seven, have met a violent end. Eight, if you count the fat man who had the coronary. And that's not even counting the nine who died up there at Little Lake Harbor."

"As far as my daughter shooting that fellow on 123—he was about to shoot *you*. She probably saved your life."

"He's still a dead body I have to explain. You would not believe the paperwork."

Jack had heard the sheriff spout off before and found it a bit tedious. So he decided to change the conversation.

"You know, Sheriff, as far as their sending someone up here to your county, to take care of the boys. I wouldn't worry too much about that. They've got the gold. I'd say it makes more sense for them to terminate the doctor and his surviving partner than to take a chance on messing with you and your deputies again."

"And then there's the matter of the boat," the sheriff interrupted.

Chapter 115

The sheriff distracted

Thankfully that was not found in my county," the sheriff continued. "There were *nine* more bodies found over there in Luce. And the harbor—the wooden pier was basically ruined."

"Kate and I had *nothing* to do with those guys on the boat, *absolutely* nothing. We have not even been in that area."

"Handler, you don't have to be pulling the trigger. You don't even have to be close by. It's just that you always seem to be the catalyst—you show up in town, and people start dropping. You've kept all my men busy just scraping up bodies. I don't think we've written a traffic ticket in two days."

"We need to keep everything in perspective, Sheriff. Especially since this thing is not yet over."

That comment caught the sheriff by surprise.

"What does that mean? Are there still some people out there that you need to kill?"

"Well, Sheriff, I sincerely hope not," Jack replied. "The thing is, we still haven't resolved the killing of the boy's father and mother. Or the nine people on that boat. Certainly you want to get to the bottom of that.

"After all, the Gordon family lived in Chippewa County. And you're the sheriff here. I think you probably consider it your job to solve that crime."

Sheriff Green grabbed Jack by the arm and stopped him: "You don't think these fellows are responsible for killing the guys on the boat? Or for blowing up the Gordon vehicle?"

"*Absolutely* not," Jack replied. "There is nothing to suggest that eliminating the boy's parents, or the people on the boat, could possibly have helped their cause. So, why would they have killed them?

"So, unless I'm missing something, I don't think the doctor's people are responsible for Gordon and his wife, or the people on Superior."

"Then, who do you like for those killings?"

"Maybe they all just committed suicide? I don't know. What do you think, Sheriff? If not for the gold, what could possibly have been a motive powerful enough to murder nine people—ten, counting the Gordon woman?"

The two men ceased talking as they continued toward the car. Red was sitting in the rear this time, so Jack got in the front.

"Think you can swing by the hospital and pick up Kate? And then drop us off on the island? My nephew needs to see how his dog's doing."

Chapter 116

Crime only half solved

The sheriff did not respond verbally, but Jack did observe that they were headed toward the hospital.

After an uncomfortably long period of silence, Jack spoke: "We still going to have that meeting tonight?"

"We just had it."

Again no one talked for a lengthy period of time.

Finally, the sheriff broke the silence.

"Handler. If you were me, what would you do next? It seems to me you're saying we've solved only half the crime. Is that right?"

Jack looked up at the sheriff in disbelief. He wasn't sure how he should respond, or if he should respond at all.

As he sat there for a few moments carefully contemplating his words, a timer went off on his cell phone. It was a reminder: "Call Pam Black."

"Excuse me, Sheriff. I've got to make a call."

* * *

(*Superior Peril* solves the mystery behind the lost gold, the fate of the Captain Titiku's Mino, and the murder of the medical emergency responder. But we still do not know who killed the nine on board Captain Gordon's Snoopy, or who murdered Robby's mother.

The next book (*Superior Intrigue*) in the "Getting to Know Jack" series answers those questions. It is due to be released in January 2014. As is the case with all the books of this series, *Superior Intrigue* will be a work of fiction.)

Epilogue

Going for the gold

The year was 1788 BC—June 10. The big lake was now tranquil, as three sixty-foot single-tree-mast Minoan vessels made their way through Whitefish Bay and then west into Lake Kitchi-Gummi—ready to begin their shipping season.

When they arrived on Isle Royale, Captain Thera of the Kasos, the lead ship of the group, inquired about the whereabouts of his friend, Captain Titiku.

Because the Mino never arrived at its homeport, Captain Thera assumed that his friend decided to spend the winter at Isle Royale or perhaps move inland with the Native American workers.

But when he was told that the Titiku set sail only a few days after he had, immediately he knew that his friend was lost at sea and certainly dead.

He inquired about the Titiku's cargo: "Did it include both the standard copper ingots as well as the special shiny ones?"

When informed that it did, his disappointment was obvious. Not only was he deeply saddened by the loss of his dear friend, he was visibly displeased with the loss of the gold.

As he waited in port for minor repairs to be made on the three ships, he requested a Native American scribe be sent him. He specified that the scribe be a member of the Ojibwa Tribe.

When the Native American scholar arrived, Captain Thera dictated a memorial tablet to his friend, Captain Titiku, the honorable captain of the great cargo ship, the Mino. He requested that the scribe translate his words into the native language, but to write it using the Minoan system of writing.

Once the tablet was finished, he, along with a select group of Minoan sailors, transported the tablet inland, and there displayed it near a large Native American settlement.

That area later came to be known as the town of Newberry, MI.

It commemorated the exploits of his friend—Titiku, the honorable captain of the ill-fated Mino.

After the end of Minoan copper mining along Lake Superior the significance of commemorative tablet, as well as the tablet itself, was lost.

IIt was not until 1896 AD that it was rediscovered, along with several pieces of Minoan art, just north of Newberry. All the artifacts were photographed, and copies were sent to the Smithsonian Institute.

Because the discovery of the Minoan civilization did not occur until the middle of the twentieth century, scholars at the Smithsonian initially declared the Newberry finds to be fakes.

And so for years the artifacts were not highly regarded, and therefore not properly stored. Therefore, they eventually deteriorated to an almost unrecognizable state.

Fortunately, the original photographs were eventually found and have since been published.

But because of the Smithsonian's original erroneous determination, the Newberry Tablet and the other Newberry artifacts were allowed to deteriorate, and some of them disappeared altogether. Fortunately, some parts of the original Newbery Tablet have been preserved, and are on display at a museum in St. Ignus, MI.

Cast of Characters
in the Getting to Know Jack Series

If you want to find out more about the series, then I would encourage you to check out the publishers website (http://www. greenwichvillageink.com).

Jack: Jack is a good man, in his way. While it is true that he kills a lot of people, it can be argued that most (if not all) of them needed killing. Occasionally a somewhat sympathetic figure comes between Jack and his goal. When that happens, Jack's goal comes first. I think the word that best sums up Jack's persona might be "expeditor." He is outcome driven—he makes things turn out the way he wants them to turn out.

For instance, if you were a single mom and a bully were stealing your kid's lunch money, you could send "Uncle Jack" to school with little Billy. Uncle Jack would have a talk with the teachers and the principal. With Jack's help, the problem would be solved. But I would not recommend that you ask him how he accomplished it. You might not like what he tells you—if he even responds.

Jack is faithful to his friends and a great father to his daughter. He is also a dangerous and tenacious adversary when situations require it.

To some extent I look to the memory of my father in determining what Jack might do in certain situations. While my father did not make a habit of killing people, like Jack, my dad was tough.

From the age of 13 my father was on his own. Working in Newberry (in Upper Michigan) as a lumberjack, he always carried a side arm. It came in handy because he was also the area's moonshiner.

But even given his hard life, I never knew my father to lie, cheat, or act in any dishonorable fashion. He was a great father and friend. Jack is like that.

Jack Handler began his career as a law enforcement officer. He married a beautiful woman of Greek descent (Beth) while working as a police officer in Chicago. She was a concert violinist and the love of his life. If you were to ask Jack about it, he would quickly tell you he married above himself. So when she was killed by bullets intended for him, he admittedly grew bitter. Kate, their daughter, was barely a year old when her mother was gunned down.

As a single father trying to raise a daughter on his own, Jack soon found that he needed to make more money than his job paid. So he went back to college and got a degree in criminal justice. Soon he was promoted to the level of sergeant in the Chicago Police Homicide Division.

With the help of a friend, he then discovered that there was much more money to be earned in the private sector. At first he began moonlighting on private security jobs. Immediate success led him to take an early retirement and obtain his private investigator license.

Because of his special talents (obtained as a former Army Ranger) and his intense dedication to problem solving, many of Jack's jobs emerged from the darker side. While Jack did take on some of the more sketchy clients, he never accepted a project simply on the basis of financial gain—he always sought out the moral high ground. Unfortunately, all too often that moral high ground morphed into quicksand.

Jack is now pushing sixty, and he has all the physical problems common to a man that age. While it is true that he remains in amazing physical condition, of late he has begun to sense his limitations.

His biggest concern right now, however, is an impending IRS audit. He isn't totally confident that it will turn out okay.

His problems stem from the purchase of half-interest in a bar in Chicago nearly two decades earlier. His partner was one of his oldest and most trusted friends.

The principal reason he made the investment was to create a cover for his private security business.

Many, if not most, of his clients insisted on paying him in cash or with some other untraceable commodity. At first he tried getting rid of the cash by paying all of his bills with it. But even though he meticulously avoided credit cards and checks, the cash continued to accumulate.

It wasn't that he was in any sense averse to paying his fair share of taxes. The problem was that if he did deposit the cash into a checking account, and subsequently included it in his filings, he would then at some point be required to explain where it had come from.

He needed an acceptable method of laundering, and his buddy's bar seemed perfect.

But it did not work out as planned. Almost one year ago the IRS decided to audit the bar.

Jack hired one of his old customers, a disbarred attorney/CPA, to see if this shady character could get the books straightened out enough for Jack to survive the audit and avoid federal prison.

The accountant knew exactly how Jack earned his money and

that the sale of a few bottles of Jack Daniels had little to do with it.

Even though his business partner and the CPA talked a good game about legitimacy, Jack still agonized about it when such thoughts barged through his mind.

Reg: In *Jack and the New York Death Mask (Death Mask)* Jack is recruited by his best friend, Reg (Reginald Black), to do a job without either man having any knowledge as to what that job might entail. Jack, out of loyalty to his friend, accepted the offer. The contract was ostensibly to assassinate a sitting president. However, instead of assisting the plot, Jack and Reg worked to thwart it. Most of this story takes place in New York City, but there are scenes in DC, Chicago, and Upstate New York. Reg is frequently mentioned throughout the series, as are Pam Black and Allison Fulbright. Pam Black is Reg's wife (he was shot at the end of *Death Mask*), and Allison is a former first lady. It was Allison who contracted Reg and Jack to assassinate the sitting president. She is currently on Pam Black's case, trying to get back the money she had paid Reg in the failed assassination scheme. Also, she still has aspirations on being president.

Kate: Kate, Jack's daughter and a New York homicide detective, is introduced early in this book. Kate is beautiful. She has her mother's olive complexion and green eyes. Her trim five-foot-eight frame, with her long auburn hair falling nicely on her broad shoulders, would seem more at home on the runway than in an interrogation room. But Kate is a seasoned New York homicide detective. In fact, she is thought by many to be on the fast track to the top—thanks in part to the unwavering support of her soon-to-retire boss, Captain Spencer.

Of course, her career was not hindered by her background in

law. Graduating Summa Cum Laude from Notre Dame at the age of twenty-one, she went on to Notre Dame Law School. She passed the Illinois Bar Exam immediately upon receiving her JD, and accepted a position at one of Chicago's most prestigious criminal law firms. While her future looked bright as a courtroom attorney, she hated defending "sleazebags."

One Saturday morning she called her father and invited him to meet her at what she knew to be his favorite coffee house. It was there, over a couple espressos, that she asked him what he thought about her taking a position with the New York Police Department. She was shocked when he immediately gave his blessing. "Kitty," he said, "you're a smart girl. I totally trust your judgment. You have to go where your heart leads. Just promise me one thing. Guarantee me that you will put me up whenever I want to visit. After all, you are my favorite daughter."

To this Kate replied with a chuckle, "Dad, I'm your only daughter. And you will always be welcome."

In *Murder on Sugar Island (Sugar)*, Jack and Kate team up to solve the murder of Alex, Jack's brother-in-law. This book takes place on Sugar Island, which is located in the northern part of Michigan's Upper Peninsula (just east of Sault Ste. Marie, MI).

A new main character is introduced in this book: Red, a red-headed thirteen-year-old who, besides being orphaned, cannot speak.

One other character of significance introduced in this book is Bill Green, the knowledgeable police officer who first appears in Joey's coffee shop. He assumes a major role in subsequent books of the series.

Red: Red has a number of outstanding characteristics. First of all, his ability to take care of himself in all situations. When his parents were killed in a fire, Red chose to live on his own instead of submitting to placement in foster care.

During the warmer months he lived in a hut he had pieced together from parts of abandoned homes, barns, and cottages, and he worked at a resort on Sugar Island. In the winter, he would take up residence in empty fishing cottages along the river.

Red's second outstanding characteristic is his loyalty. When put to the test, Red would rather sacrifice his life than see his friends hurt. In *Sugar,* Red works together with Jack and Kate to solve the mystery behind the killing of Jack's brother-in-law Alex. Alex was the owner of the resort where Red worked, and he shared a very significant relationship with the boy.

The third thing about Red that make's him stand out is his inability to speak. As the result of a traumatic event in his life, his voice box was damaged, resulting in his disability. Before Jack and Kate entered his life, Red communicated only through an improvised sign system, and various grunts.

When Kate introduced him to a cell phone, and texting, Red's life changed dramatically.

In *Superior Peril (Peril)* and *Superior Intrigue (Intrigue),* which will be available in the spring of 2014, all of the above characters play major roles. Plus there were some new colorful characters introduced in those two books.

Additional comments about the Jack Handler series

Finally, there is a new author who will challenge the likes of Michael Connelly and David Baldacci. — Island Books

If you like James Patterson and Michael Connelly, you'll love Michael Carrier. Carrier has proven that he can hang with the best of them. It has all of the great, edge-of-your-seat action and suspense that you'd expect in a good thriller, and it kept me guessing to the very end. Fantastic read with an awesome detective duo—I couldn't put it down! — Katie

Don't read Carrier at the beach or you are sure to get sunburned. I did. I loved the characters. It was so descriptive you feel like you know everyone. Lots of action—always something happening. I love the surprise twists. All my friends are reading it now because I wouldn't talk to them until I finished it so they knew it was good. Carrier is my new favorite author! — Sue

Thoroughly enjoyed this read — kept me turning page after page! Good character development and captivating plot. Had theories but couldn't quite solve the mystery without reading to the end. Highly recommended for readers of all ages. — Terry

Top Shelf Murder Mystery—Riveting. Being a Murder-Mystery "JUNKIE" this book is definitely a keeper ... can't put it down ... read it again type of book...and it is very precise to the lifestyles in Upper Michigan. Very well researched. I am a resident of this area. His attention to detail is great. I have to rate this book in the same class or better than authors Michael Connelly, James Patterson, and

Steve Hamilton. — Shelldrakeshores

Being a Michigan native, I was immediately drawn to this book. Michael Carrier is right in step with his contemporaries James Patterson and David Baldacci. I am anxious to read more of his work. I highly recommend this one! — J. Henningsen

A fast and interesting read. Michael ends each chapter with a hook that makes you want to keep reading. The relationship between father and daughter is compelling. Good book for those who like a quick moving detective story where the characters often break the "rules" for the greater good! I'm looking forward to reading the author's next book. — Flower Lady

Move over Patterson, I now have a new favorite author, Jack and his daughter make a great tag team, great intrigue, and diversions. I have a cabin on Sugar Island and enjoyed the references to the locations. I met the author at Joey's coffee shop up on the hill,(the real live Joey) great writer, good stuff. I don't usually finish a book in the course of a week, but read this one in two sittings so it definitely had my attention. I am looking forward to the next installment. Bravo. — Northland Press

My husband is not a reader— he probably hasn't read a book since his last elementary school book report was due. But ... he took my copy of Murder on Sugar Island to deer camp and read the whole thing in two days. After he recommended the book to me, I read it— being the book snob that I am, I thought I had the whole plot figured out within the first few pages, but a few chapters later, I was mystified once again. After that surprise ending, we ordered the other two Getting to Know Jack books. — Erin W.

I enjoyed this book very much. It was very entertaining, and the story unfolded in a believable manner. Jack Handler is a likable character. But you would not like to be on his wrong side. Handler made that very clear in Jack and the New York Death Mask. This book (Murder on Sugar Island) was the first book in the Getting to Know Jack series that I read. After I read Death Mask, I discovered just how tough Jack Handler really was.

I heard that Carrier is about to come out with another Jack Handler book—a sequel to Superior Peril. I will read it the day it becomes available. And I will undoubtedly finish it before I go to bed. If he could write them faster, I would be happy.

Actually, I'll take what I can get. — Deborah M.

I thoroughly enjoyed this book. I could not turn the pages fast enough. I am not sure it was plausible, but I love the characters. I highly recommend this book and look forward to reading more by Michael Carrier. — Amazon Reader

An intense thrill ride!! — Mario

Michael Carrier has knocked it out of the park — John

Left on the edge of my seat after the last book, I could not wait for the next chapter to unfold and Mike Carrier did not disappoint! I truly feel I know his characters better with each novel and I especially like the can-do/will-do attitude of Jack. Keep up the fine work, Mike and may your pen never run dry! — SW

The Handlers are at it again, with the action starting on Sugar Island, I am really starting to enjoy the way the father daughter and now Red are working through the mind of Mike Carrier. The entire family, plus a few more are becoming the reason for the new sheriff's increased body count and antacid intake. The twists and turns we have come to expect are all there and then some. I'm looking for the next installment already. — Northland Press

Map of Area

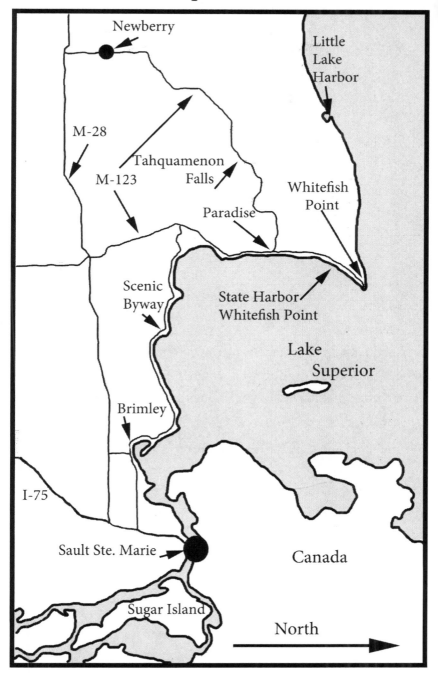

The Inscrutable Puzzle

In *Jack and the New York Death Mask* (first book in the "Getting to Know Jack" series) Jack's close friend, Reginald (Reg) Black, left this bloody cryptogram for Jack to find when he (Reg) was shot in a successful attempt to free Kate (Jack's daughter) from her Eastern European abductors.

At the time he discovered it (in Reg's blood-soaked trousers) Jack knew it was significant, and that Reg had intended it for him to find. However, the first night that it was in his possession it was stolen from Jack's hotel room. The culprit: two of former First Lady Allison Fulbright's operatives. Fortunately, Jack had copied the puzzle, and taken an image of it before the theft.

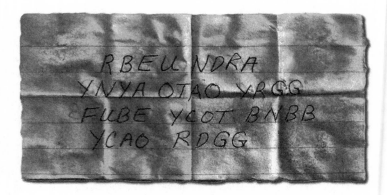

Now Allison is reentering the picture. She wants to Exhume Reg's body from Calvary Cemetery in Queens, New York. Jack does not know her motivation, nor does Pam Black, Reg's widow.

Could it have something to do with the plaintext behind this cryptogram?

So far no one has been able to decipher the puzzle. Could it point to the location that Reg hid the one hundred million dollars in gold that he had received from Allison as payment for the assassination of a sitting president? Is that why Allison is so adamant about digging Reg up? As of right now, we don't know.

Some smart people have declared this puzzle to be inscrutable—unsolvable. But, we know better than that. There is no such thing as an unsolvable puzzle.

There is a key (of sorts) included with the puzzle in *Jack and the New York Death Mask*.

My fascination with the Minoan Newberry Tablet

Please understand that I do not pretend to be an expert on the ancient Minoan script. However, my background provides me with a better than pedestrian understanding of it.

As a graduate student at New York University in the 70s (majoring in Semitic languages), I had the privilege of studying under a truly wonderful scholar—Dr. Cyrus Gordon.

One of the courses I took from him was a study of Minoan. He had some years earlier published an amazing monograph on Minoan Linear "A". It was titled "Evidence for the Minoan Language." His theory was that the ancient Greek culture was based on Semitic roots. He developed his premise on the fact that certain Minoan Linear "A" writings from Crete looked to be Semitic in origin, and, since Minoan Linear "A" preceded the classical Greek period, then the Greek language/culture must therefore have been founded on Semitic origins.

While his theory has been challenged by subsequent scholarship, I found the arguments he presented to be entirely fascinating.

So, when I first laid my eyes on the 1898 image of the Newberry Tablet, I believed it to be a Minoan tablet, or at least a very good forgery. And given the date of its discovery, I had little doubt that it was the genuine article.

Of course, the narrative I created in *Superior Peril* regarding the origin and intent of the Newberry Tablet was totally fictional. However, I believe it was quite plausible.

Not only were Minoans accomplished seafarers, but during this period they were the only people who had the fleet of transport ships necessary to navigate the waters not only throughout the Middle East and Europe, but even as far as the rivers of North and South America.

However, the secret of their success was based more on what they didn't have, than on what they did. The Minoans never developed an army, and therefore never posed a threat. That's why they were allowed to survive for so long. Basically they worked for whoever happened to be in power at the time.

One of the necessary characteristics developed by every group of people that seek to excel in the shipping business is the ability to communicate with all of its trading partners.

But, we have no reason to think that there was during this period a common language that was understood throughout the world—that is, there was no *lingua franca*. This would be particularly true with regard to all the ports along the Mississippi River and the St. Lawrence Seaway—both of which some archaeologists hold to be well-established Minoan shipping lanes.

Therefore, I think it's quite possible that what the Minoans did was to apply their syllabic form of writing to all the various languages that they encountered. That way any member of their maritime personnel could communicate with suppliers and customers by simply pronouncing the characters as they would if they were reading a Minoan document. It would sound enough like the native language that it could be understood by the native speakers. This practice (of phonetically converting a document from one script to another) is called *transliteration*.

If this did happen, then it would make Minoan the *scripta franca* during the Bronze Age. (It could also help explain some of Cyrus Gordon's suppositions regarding Minoan.)

Furthermore, if that is correct, then I suspect that the same principle just might be applicable to understanding the Newberry Tablet. That is, I think it is possible that the tablet was written using Minoan syllabic symbols, but that the language was actually Native American (Ojibemowin?). If so, then the contents would likely have to do with business—it would be a bill of lading, or something similar.

That is, of course, just my supposition—I have no proof for it. However, as far the translation attempts published at this time are concerned, I have not seen any that I would consider acceptable, much less definitive.

That, too, is just my opinion.

(Note: I am aware of the current degraded condition of the physical artifact on display. I could not begin to document its authenticity (that must be left to the real scholars). My thoughts are based solely on the 1898 image of the Newberry Tablet, and on my study of Minoan. That having been said, one should keep in mind that a History Channel documentary recently authenticated the Newberry Tablet.

Of course, when it comes to matters like this, I always defer to the words of Michel de Montaigne, *Que sais-je:* "[But] what do I know?" Regarding this admission, I'm sure that there is no shortage of scholars who would applaud.)

Made in the USA
Lexington, KY
22 July 2018